JEAN

JEAN

A Novel

Madeleine Dunnigan

W. W. NORTON & COMPANY
Independent Publishers Since 1923

Jean is a work of fiction. Although it is loosely inspired by an event in my family history that predates my own birth, all of the usual rules of fiction apply: no person, place or event in the book should be understood as a literal depiction of any actual person, place, or circumstance, and none should be construed as real.

Printed in the United States of America
First Edition

For information about special discounts for bulk purchases, please contact W. W. Norton Special Sales at specialsales@wwnorton.com or 800-233-4830

Manufacturing by Lakeside Book Company
Book design by Chris Welch
Production manager: Ramona Wilkes

ISBN 978-1-324-10564-0

W. W. Norton & Company, Inc., 500 Fifth Avenue, New York, NY 10110
www.wwnorton.com

W. W. Norton & Company Ltd., 15 Carlisle Street, London W1D 3BS

Authorized EU representative: EAS, Mustamäe tee 50, 10621 Tallinn, Estonia

1 0 9 8 7 6 5 4 3 2 1

For my family.

I wasn't truly myself except the moment I was running away . . .

—Patrick Modiano, *In the Café of Lost Youth*, (trans. Euan Cameron)

I

England, 1976

HE IS VERY, VERY LUCKY TO BE HERE—SO SAYS DAVID LARKIN, the headmaster.

It is luck that Jean thinks about while looking out of the window in the headmaster's office, where, down by the lake, he can see the dark smudges of boys racing along the pontoon, and how, really, he so often has the opposite.

It was unlucky, for example, that Samuel should sit next to him in biology. Unlucky that Samuel, who has sinus problems, should sneeze as he turned to face Jean, and unlucky that the spray—thousands, millions, even billions of bacteria—should hit Jean on his neck, his cheek, his lips.

What to do when faced with such a situation? When all the

forces of the world conspire against you. Fight back, of course. Like Bruce Lee says, you make your own luck.

So that was what Jean did. He hit Samuel—just as Samuel had hit him with his fist of germs—square in the mouth. Lord of Unluck.

Through the window three pink smudges disappear into the dazzlingly blue water.

Jean, David says.

And that is why Jean now sits before this balding man, liver spotted across his forehead, skin shiny with sweat. If Jean had to guess, he would say David Larkin is about fifty. Although he doesn't behave like most old people. He insists the boys call him Davey—all the teachers go by their Christian names at Compton Manor. He encourages the boys to be outside as much as possible, exploring the *fertile land of this blessed place*. Once he brought in a box of live frogs for the boys to dissect.

He is, in other words, weird. Like Rosa. With her short hair and overalls, she is Rosa, never mum, and if Jean should even think of calling her mother, well then. As if it isn't bad enough that she works, she is an *artist*. Talking politics with a crowd of students around the dinner table, a cloud of smoke above them, shouting at Jean to join, swearing into the early hours of the morning. Although David (Jean cannot bring himself to call him Davey) would never swear. He is, despite—or is it because of—running a school of half-wild boys, a Good Christian.

Jean, David says. Are you listening?

The headmaster sits behind a large mahogany desk. Behind him shelves lined with books—Nietzsche, Jung, Krishnamurti, *The Years of Awakening*—are squeezed between the narrow windows that encircle the room. His office is at the base of one of the turrets. It is nothing like any headmaster's office Jean has been in before (and he has been in a few). The classrooms are strange: dark rooms in the depths of the building, surrounded by tapestries and old paintings, or light-filled spaces with high-arched ceilings where the boys sit at wooden tables, facing each other. There is a smoking room with green leather furniture and a billiard room with a large open fire and glass-covered bookshelves. There are other rooms, too, hidden in the folds of the building's expanse, filled with shapes under ghostly white sheets, dust particles hanging in the air or, otherwise, locked.

Jean knows the history: The building was erected by wealthy cloth merchants in the seventeenth century and enlarged in the eighteenth by a bachelor dandy, who had great plans for it. Alongside the formal parterres, the fountain with the gravity-defying Diver statue, the Tuscan arches with their jasmine, the ornamental garden with its roses, peonies, and tall, exotic plants, the boating pond, and the folly, there was meant to be a grand topiary maze, a Japanese sand garden, and a waterfall. But the bachelor died quite suddenly and the project lost steam. Forty years later, the great-great-nephew leased the place to his whacky chum, David Larkin (they read history at Trinity College, Cambridge, together), who reopened it as a remedial school for boys. David likes to tell this story as an example of the boys' good fortune, but it simply reminds Jean that he does not belong here. Jean is glad there is no maze and no waterfall; instead, the wildflower meadow, the field, the lake.

David rests his hands on the desk, a bead of sweat poised on his forehead.

I take the welfare of my boys, all my boys, very seriously. We are a family, he says.

Jean thinks of Rosa the morning after, screaming at him in the kitchen, a plate flying toward his head.

You know you're expected to take care of others.

Rosa weeping on the sofa as she bandages the cut on his forehead.

You know that you're not, David says, his voice suddenly low, Expected to punch a boy.

Rosa in the garden squinting in the sun, sketching furiously as Jean lies in the grass half asleep.

Don't you? David says.

Behind David, nestled among the books, are the school photographs. There are four in total. Jean scans them, searching for this year's, 1976. It is the one with the most people: sixty boys, the sum of the student body, and ten teachers, plus David, Matron, Cook, Nurse, and the gardener. The subjects are arranged in a disorganised mass on the gravel drive in front of the school. The boys: cutoff jeans, bell-bottoms, patterned shirts, dirty white T-shirts, vests, bomber jackets, Adidas pumps, Wellington work boots (but mostly, bare feet), shaggy and unkempt hair, arms slung around each other, some shouting. The teachers look more traditional in Oxford shirts and knitted vests, although there is one, Charles Burrows, the English teacher, who wears a tight purple shirt and flares and has one foot balanced across his knee like the boys on the bench next to him. Jean scans the photo but cannot see himself there.

David loves to talk about the *band of brothers* that is the school. Loves to use words like *family*, and *responsibility*, and *care*. But Jean can tell David is frustrated—that Jean has frustrated him by not buying his crap—from the way his top lip twitches.

For God's sake, Jean.

Jean is surprised and, also, a little proud; David only blasphemes when desperate.

I don't need to remind you that it is precisely because of fee-paying boys like Samuel that you're here.

It is Jean's turn to blush.

Whoever loves his brother lives in the light, and there is nothing in him to make him stumble, David says. *But whoever hates his brother is in the darkness, and he walks about in darkness. He does not know where he is going because the darkness has blinded him.*

Jean hates David Larkin then. Hates him for bringing up money and bringing up the Bible. For reminding Jean that he is poor and that he is Jewish.

Noises from outside filter in, the shrieks of boys by the pond, somewhere else, a guitar, but inside the room, silence. Jean holds David's gaze. He will not be the one to break it. David wipes his sweaty brow with a burgundy handkerchief.

Look, he says. Meet me halfway here. Leave it out of the classroom, OK. I don't want to hear about it again.

Jean says nothing. Blinks.

There are bigger things to worry about, David says. Have you thought about what you want to do next year? I know exams seem like a waste of time. Believe me, if it was up to me, we wouldn't have any, but the fact is you've got to sit them. You've got to think about your future.

Jean picks at a scab on his knee. It begins to bleed. He waits, but David has run out of steam. After what Jean considers a suitably long amount of time he says: Can I go?

David sighs. Fine. Fine.

Jean shares his dorm room with four others. It is mixed years to *foster a sense of collegiate fraternity*, as David says. In reality, the younger boys are the older boys' fags. Not Jean's—even though he is seventeen and one of the oldest. No, Jean occupies a kind of grey zone outside of the school ecosystem; he likes to think of himself on a cloud, levitating.

David says brother, Jean says distant cousin at best.

The dorm is a bomb site. Clothes, records, books, and general crap—model aeroplanes, empty bottles, a whole branch, some pebbles, and three empty peach tins—scatter the floor. Clearly the servants haven't been doing their jobs. Classes finished ages ago and even though there are still hours of sunlight left, Jean doesn't want to spend a minute more inside.

Jean has heard David's family spiel, or a version of it, many times. When he has been sent to David's office for misbehaviour or when David gives informal sermons to the common room. Come into the light. Precisely what Jean is desperate to do.

He finds his way across the sea of junk to his bed. Somehow his things are everywhere too, even though he didn't partake in whatever went on. Panic grips him as he rifles through his trunk, dissipating to dread. But it's there: his old Allenburys Blackcurrant Cough Pastilles tin. Tucked underneath the games kit that gets little to no use.

As he heads to the woods, he passes Percy, Theo, Tom, and Hugo coming back from the boating pond. Their hair is wet and they are shirtless. They are the boys who are good at sport and who speak in loud, posh voices, walking around as if they own the school. In some ways, they do; certainly they pay for it.

Percy's mother runs a small hotel dynasty in the Mediterranean; although Theo's father is a cab driver—an immigrant no less, arriving from Port Maria on the SS *Almanzora*—he served in the RAF before that, and Theo's mother is an American heiress to a fortune made from the invention of the dimmer switch; Tom's father used to be one of the country's largest mine owners, now he runs a chicken farm in Shropshire; and Hugo, the ringleader, Hugo was born on some estate where little Hugos have been born for centuries, living off the interest on their money. Hugo, Percy, Theo, and Tom are in their final year like Jean (there are only seven last years in total). Unlike Jean, though, in so many ways. Rosa again, paint-covered, the German accent becoming stronger with each glass of wine. This merry band of brothers, David's saved souls. The thought makes Jean smile and it is this that Hugo picks up on.

Telling yourself jokes again, Yid? I've got one: Knock, Knock.

As Hugo swings, Jean swerves, and in doing so makes eye contact with Tom. It is nearly imperceptible, but there is a slight raise of the eyebrow, a twitch of the lip.

And then Jean is gone, tripping down the field with Hugo shouting after him: Anyone in there?

Had the strangest dream last night, Tom says and passes Jean the joint. I was at school, down in the lower field, and I was riding a giant rabbit. It looked like a horse or a bus or a tank, you know like the Russians', but actually it was one of Charlie's rabbits. Except it wasn't.

Tom stops, out of breath, the last of the smoke escaping in short coughs.

Weird, right?

Tom gets out of breath easily. He has epilepsy, which means he takes six pills a day, two each with breakfast, lunch, and dinner. He should be *careful* he told Jean when, a few weeks ago, he came up to him at the farm that sits adjacent to the school. He should be careful, except that Tom is on the football team and does cross country and can often be seen chasing younger boys down the corridors, or climbing the walls to steal the hanging medieval hunting horn, or driving Matron's old Austin 1100 through the mud-drenched fields, or dancing wildly at the school disco, lithe chest pumping as it did when he ran through the meadow, down to the lake, where he now stands with Jean, smoking, his pale legs reflecting the water.

Tom is in charge of the chickens at the farm (after all, it runs in the family; the boys call him King Cock). Jean is usually with the pigs but since Tom came up to him, he has been upgraded to chickens. The feel of the warm, fragile egg in the palm of his hand. The smell of the straw and the soft clucking of the birds.

Tom is shorter than Jean, who is one of the tallest at over six foot. Tom's hair is brown where Jean's is blond, his skin pale, Jean's dark. Jean's nose is a lumpen thing that follows from his cheekbones whereas Tom's is smooth, straight, as if it has been cast from marble. Tom has eyes like a cat. Brown, although Jean has never looked in them long enough to know if they are dark, light, or hazel. If there are flecks in the irises, if there is a rim around the edge. He imagines they are like the forest floor. Earthy, textured, full of rot. Jean's eyes are blue; Rosa calls them galaxies. There is a scar between Jean's eyebrows and another below his bottom lip. Tom won't have noticed them, though. But Jean has noticed the freckles on Tom's nose and cheeks, and a smattering of pink spots along his cheekbones. Sometimes yellow heads erupt. He wants to squeeze them.

Jean looks away, takes a drag. Dreams are stupid, he says.

Jean did not know why Tom came up to him three weeks ago. Jean was in the back of the pig pen, sweat stinging his eyes as he shovelled shit, wondering if he could survive without food for eighteen hours a day like Buddhists, when he noticed Tom standing there. Jean's impulse was to crouch, shitty fork held out in front of him in defence—Jean had been at Compton Manor for almost two years, and he could count on one hand the number of times Tom had spoken to him—but he forced himself to remain standing, to lean on the fork and look at Tom from under his fringe. Tom, hands in pockets, toed the straw, told Jean that he had epilepsy, that he should be careful. He asked Jean what part of London he was from, did he like Black Sabbath or The Clash, could he drive, and then: What's wrong with you?

At Compton Manor the boys have lots of different problems. There is one who shouts swear words and one who doesn't speak at all. There are some who can't look you in the eye and several who have asthma, and even one boy who is in a wheelchair. Jean feels sorry for him; once, his chair went missing, taken while he was on the toilet. He sat for five hours before calling for help. Then there are boys like Jean who, on the outside, look normal. Whose illness is trapped somewhere beneath the layers of his skin.

Isn't that precisely why Rosa sent Jean to Compton Manor? There was, of course, the specific event, the original crime—at Jean's last school he stuck a compass in another boy's face—and then there were all the events, all the crimes, that led up to it. Jean, eight years old, smashes everything glass in the house; or twelve on a Cornish beach, destroying another family's picnic. Thirteen and a barn is on fire. Fifteen and the long, stupid neck of a peacock lies limply in his hands. The boy at his last school was lucky not to lose an eye, the headmaster reported. It was bad, even Jean can admit that (still, the prick deserved it), but not so bad that it should have resulted in his immediate removal from normal education. It was the preceding events, all the things he had done throughout his childhood and now his adolescence, leading up to that point and which created a sense—for Rosa, and for Jean—that there truly was something irredeemably wrong with him that caused her, finally, to send him to Compton Manor, aka House of Nutters.

Once, when he was younger, a lady doctor with glasses asked him a different version of the same question. Where does it come from, she said. All this anger? He didn't know what to say. Where does the sea come from? From the rivers, the streams, the springs and deeper—from the rocks, the sediment, the fossils, the molten centre of the earth.

Of course, when Tom asked Jean what was wrong with him, Jean did not say any of this. Rather, he thought back to how the wheelchair was found submerged in the lake, one wheel broken, how he had seen Tom and Hugo shortly after, sniggering by the dormitories, and gripped the fork tighter. Then Tom smiled, colouring slightly, and said he heard Jean might have something to smoke.

Right, Tom says now, inspecting the joint. Don't dreams mean something though? Like what your man says. That German fella.

Freud, Jean says, blowing smoke through his nostrils. He was Austrian.

Tom has sought Jean out sporadically these last few weeks, sometimes once a day, sometimes less. Jean has shown Tom how to smoke—how to crumble the cannabis and mix it with the tobacco, the soft pinch and swift roll. Jean doesn't mind that Tom is using him. He has enough to share. And it is better to smoke with someone, sometimes. At least, Jean likes smoking with Tom. Tom has shown Jean how to fish: how to tie the tackle, wrapping the line around itself, wetting the end, and pulling it through. How to attach the bait, piercing the soft worm in two places, so it doesn't slip off, and how to cast, whipping his arm back so the line reaches far across the water, a trail of expanding circles beneath.

You're secretly in love with rabbits, Jean says.

Tom screws up his face. Fuck off.

Outside of these moments together, though, Tom slides back into the slipstream of friends and football and classes. He doesn't ignore Jean, no, he will lift a hand if they pass in the corridor, nod to him in the dinner hall, but Tom has so many other friends. Tom likes people. He likes to laugh and slap boys' backs. He likes good, solid, English fun, loud singing and ale and hunting and billiards and lots of things Jean has no idea about and no interest in.

Jean doesn't mind that Tom doesn't talk to him during the day. Jean has his manifesto to work on, his meditation, his music. He has the problems of the universe to figure out. Jean would be lying if he said he had not noticed Tom before; but truthfully he thought Tom was a bit of a wanker, dismissing him as one of those posh boys Jean never would, and didn't want to, be friends with. These days there is a tightness in his chest and an increase in his pulse when the bell marks the end of school, the day draws to a close, and he knows he might see Tom.

Jean passes back the joint and bends toward the water. It is soft and cool.

On the evenings that he does see Tom, they are silent at first; slowly, Tom will talk. Almost to himself. About growing up in the north in a house with grounds larger than the school. About how he shot and skinned his first rabbit when he was only ten (something all the boys learn at Compton Manor, and which Tom is so good at he has been promoted to teacher); how his father has a rifle from the First World War in the basement; and how in the lake on their land, there are eels. Dark, long, slimy things like dismembered arms with sharp teeth that will nip you if you fall in. About his brother, George, who owns a sports car and drives fast down narrow country lanes blasting The Beatles.

Jean likes the sound of it, except for The Beatles, who, he has had to tell Tom, are shit. Tom has told Jean that this part of Sussex, where the school sits, is native to over at least thirty different apple trees, offering him the fruit he nicked from the kitchen garden. And it was Tom who, when the headless pigeon carcass fell from the sky, told Jean that peregrine falcons were roosting on the school roof, eating the brains of smaller birds.

And now, Jean realises, Tom has told him about his dreams. He smiles, imagining Tom riding one of Charles Burrows' rabbits. The rabbits the English teacher keeps are Angora. They are his personal rabbits, not for killing or skinning but for making yarn, which he does late at night in the common room in front of the telly.

Jean has told Tom things too. How in London you can go to a party and stay out all night, following the movement of feet; how upstairs there are the punks and downstairs there are the Rastas, and how it's fine until the skinheads show up. Jean told Tom how in Wing Chun you use your opponent's force against him; you must protect your centre and establish a bridge, a point of contact between the arms, because information travels quicker through touch than by sight. If your opponent retreats, you must follow, keeping close. If the force is too great, then you must move, restructuring the fight, so you are always poised, perfectly balanced. It is not about the force of your punch but about the speed and mass of your body.

Like a bird, Tom had said. Yes, like a bird. But if a skin has a knife, it is better to just run.

Jean has told Tom how Bruce Lee trained in Wing Chun, became a master, and developed his own practice, taking the best bits from different combat forms and combining them with his own philosophy. Jean explained that Tom needed to awaken his inner warrior, let go of attachments, and be open to the world around him. Tom looked at Jean funny then.

It was late, most of the boys were asleep, and they had smoked a particularly strong joint. Usually, the sight of Tom's smirk would make Jean shut up, but the grass made him reckless.

It's like the moon, Jean said. The moon is, like, truth.

Tom shifted his weight next to Jean.

And your finger, Jean said, pointing. Your finger is all the human shit.

My finger is shit? Tom said.

No, the stuff in your head.

What you saying about my head?

Jean tried again. It's about being stuck on what's not important. He waggled his finger. Just past it, there's the moon. That's what you want to focus on. The stars, the sky, the moon.

Jean sighed. He wasn't used to talking so much. He probably sounded like a freak.

Later, when they walked back to school, the moon was bright at their backs and they followed their shadows flung out before them, darker than the night, across the fields.

Tom didn't call Jean a freak. Instead, he called him *Master Blondie*. Jean laughed, but secretly he was pleased. He didn't tell Tom that he had copied everything about the moon and the finger from his favourite Bruce Lee film, *Enter the Dragon*.

Tom is more open now when Jean speaks about communism, even though his dad is a *businessman*, even though Commies are worse than Jews, no offence—Jean may not look Jewish with his ice-blond hair and blue eyes, but his surname gives him away—and a threat to democracy and the reason we might have a third world war, except this time it won't be a few Krauts bombing London but total, complete annihilation.

Hopefully it happens before exams, Jean said.

There are two months left of school. In the summer they will sit their O-levels—Jean has just turned seventeen; he is one year older than Tom and the others on account of all the school he missed—then what? Jean could go back to London, Holland Park, the King's Road, parties, music, living. But this also means going back to Rosa. Jean might not know what he wants to do with his life, but he knows he does not want to go home. He doesn't need to decide now, though. There are still two months, a whole summer, and the end of this joint to finish.

He takes one of the last burning drags and passes it back to Tom.

Was thinking about writing a letter to Mao, he says.

Oh yeah?

Yeah.

The lake they stand by sits in the base of the shallow valley that runs along the edge of the land, at least a fifteen-minute walk from the school. It is wide, Jean reckons six hundred metres, maybe more, and its edges are dominated by tall, sharp reeds and soft, sludgy mud. The boating pond is closer to the school, with a long pier the boys can dive from and for these reasons—distance and water access—it is the preferred location for most, meaning Tom and Jean can go to the lake without fear of disturbance. It is a hot day in early June. The air by the water vibrates with a low-frequency hum—dragonflies skim the water's surface, grasshoppers lunge—dampened by the heat of the sun.

Thought he might send us books, Jean says.

Us?

What?

I'm sure Chairman Mao has better things to do.

Jean squints at the sun; when he looks at the lake again, there is a dark hole in his vision, like a burnt photograph, that grows as he turns his head, eating up the water, the bank on the far side, the dense woods beyond, the buzzing insects.

What are you doing after?

Tom lies back in the long grass. By his head a cluster of buttercups glows yellow.

Dunno. Go for a drive. Lodge a branch in Rory's wheelchair.

No, after this. Jean says, lying next to him. School.

My pa wants me to join the business.

I'm going to China.

Oh yeah?

Jean only just thought of it now, but it makes sense. He will get away from Rosa and go to the source, learn martial arts, or become a Buddhist. He wishes he'd thought of that when David asked him. Jean always thinks of things too late.

Won't your ma be pissed? Tom says.

The last time Jean was home Rosa had thrown a glass of orange juice at him when he'd returned in the early hours of the morning. She had been awake all night waiting for him, she said through tears. This wasn't a hostel; if he wanted to come home at any hour of the day, he could go elsewhere. So he had. For three days, sleeping on the floor of a squat in Westbourne Grove. Eventually he got hungry and smelly and went home again. That time Rosa didn't throw anything. She grabbed him so hard it almost hurt. Almost. He extricated himself and ran a bath, and she hovered outside the door. That night she climbed into his bed, and he felt her shaking while she held him.

It's not that Rosa is bad all the time—not like she shouts and swears and throws things every day—but even when she is good, she is bad. Coming into his room without knocking, dragging him on school trips with her students, making him eat things he doesn't like. She calls too often. Like yesterday after dinner, when it was another perfect evening and he was dying to get to the lake, but instead he'd had to go to David's office where the telephone is.

Hello? Jean?

Hi.

Darling, I've been trying to get hold of you. Where have you been?

You know where I am.

You haven't called me back. You haven't written.

I'm fine, he said.

Remember to eat lots of fruit.

David was sitting at his desk reading a magazine and smoking. Jean pressed the telephone close to his ear hoping Rosa's voice would not reach the headmaster. The door to the office was open and occasionally boys passed, peering in with open curiosity. Jean spoke as little as possible. He did not want the others to know his mother was alone, had never married and that she was now talking to him about interior decoration. She spoke for several minutes about the rooms she was going to switch around in the house, how he would be in the back room, and how she was extending her studio. Jean couldn't concentrate. David flicked a page of the magazine, but Jean had the feeling he was not reading it.

It's very difficult, Rosa said, To have a conversation with someone who only speaks in monosyllables.

David's eyes met Jean's and Jean turned toward the door.

I am not one of your brain-dead friends, Jean. I am your *mother.*

God he wanted to hang up the phone, but he knew that if he did, Rosa would call back; and if he wasn't careful—too late. She was shouting now. Telling him he could forget about the radio he wanted for his birthday, which she'd already bought at an eye-watering expense.

Tom flashed past, paused, jerked his head in invitation. When Jean didn't respond, pressing the phone closer to his ear, Tom's expression turned from conspiratorial to confused. How Jean longed to say something to him then. Instead he looked away, Rosa saying that even though he had a school grant there were expenses to be paid, expenses she worked herself to the bone for, just so he could get a good education.

Nah, Jean says now, Rosa won't care.

Lucky, Tom says. My ma would go through the roof if I upped sticks.

Why don't you?

What?

Come with me. Jean squints at the sky. A gauze of cloud is spread across its surface, mottling the blue white. If you want.

To China?

Why not?

I never thought about it.

Jean stands, shaking out legs that are fizzy with pins and needles. He crouches by the lake, near the reeds. It is dark here. The space between the long grass and water is sheltered from the sun, making dark, cool patches of damp.

Look, Jean says, extending his hands.

Cupped between them the frog sits, its body pumping. The frog is beautiful, dark green with a fine sheen. Jean feels the throbbing body, its beating heart. He tightens his grip. He wants to crush the frog, to see its eyes bulge and pop, its brains ooze out, thick and grey and sticky.

Careful.

Jean thrusts the frog at Tom—What *is* wrong with him?—swapping it for the joint. He watches Tom stroke the animal—two fingers sliding down its back. The frog is very still, blinking up at Jean as if it knows, *knows*, what Jean wants to do. Blinking at Jean from two colourless pools of darkness. Jean turns away and rubs his hands on his thighs to get rid of the frog-feel.

See here, Tom says.

Their foreheads almost touch and the space in between makes Jean's face tingle. The cool, dark patches between the reeds. The freckles on Tom's nose match the dots on the frog's back. The small body pulsates gently in Tom's hands. Green slides into blue, then yellow, then silver.

It's a pool frog, Tom says.

Jean can feel the heat between their faces, smell the weed and tobacco and lunch on Tom's breath.

They're rare.

Cool.

Frogs have accents too.

Jean can feel a slight breeze, or touch, from Tom's eyelashes.

I wonder what this fella sounds like to all the other frogs.

Hopefully not like you, Jean says, his voice wobbling in a funny, high-pitched way.

Tom bends down to release the frog and in the space where his face had been there is suddenly nothing. The darkness between their foreheads, hot and close, is replaced by sunlight and breeze.

Then, from where he is crouched on the ground, Tom says: Why not? I could do with a trip.

It takes Jean a minute to realise what Tom means, and when he does, a prickling begins in his chest, spreading, like so many ants, down his arms and legs. Imagine, Tom and him, backpacks on, trekking through dark green forests side by side; or he, Jean, slightly in front, showing Tom the way. They stop and take a drink from the canteen, wipe the sweat from their foreheads. At night they camp under the stars wrapped in their coats, a dying fire whispers beside them.

OK.

Tom's shorts have ridden up, revealing the pale, untanned

skin of his upper thigh. Tom stands, looks at Jean. The proximity of their bodies means Jean can see his eyes, really see them, for the first time. They are lighter than he imagined—amber, like honey pouring from a spoon, late-afternoon light in the classroom, the underside of a butterfly's wing. The prickling is unbearable.

Jean takes off his T-shirt and wades into the water.

Where you going?

The soft mud beneath his feet, the scratching reeds at his calves, the rim of water that rises around his legs, his waist. He ducks under and then there is the blankness beneath. Jean's breath leaves him in bubbles. He is immersed in the water, free from the algae and mulch. As he swims farther, the darkness behind his eyes deepens. The freckles on Tom's nose, the dip in his throat, the milky skin of his thigh, the soft yellow of his eyes slip away and are replaced by the safety of the lake.

Tom will come to China. He repeats it like a mantra in his mind, the water spreading infinitely around him. Something feathery scales his leg, his arms strain against the pressure. Above, the faint heat of the sun penetrates the surface. Below, it is both thinner and denser. Then another thought appears, breaking Jean's stride and almost making him choke: Jean won't get his O-levels, he won't finish school, and after this summer, he will never see Tom again. He hits a cold patch and his mind stills, the thought disappearing in a stream of bubbles that tickle his cheeks. He pushes deeper, toward the coolness, the weight around his ears increasing, away from the light and into the dark.

II

ONE WEEK LATER, JEAN IS IN ENGLISH.

Glory be to God for dappled things, Charles Burrows says. *For skies of couple-colour as a brinded cow.* What might Hopkins mean by these lines?

There are lots of strange things about Compton Manor, but Charles Burrows is strangest of all.

He is young, only a few years older than Jean himself (he cannot be older than twenty-six, surely). Charles wears bright, patterned shirts that cling to his body, three-piece suits in red and brown and orange, and oval, purple-tinted spectacles. His hair is always combed, moustache just so. He rarely goes farther than the manicured lawn outside, and never to the farm. In the evenings, he can be found in his turmeric-coloured robe in front of *Fawlty Towers* stroking an Angora rabbit in his lap with one hand and smoking a cigarette with the other. The hand will move across the animal's trembling body, fingers clawing, nails pulling up fine white fur. Charles will ash his cigarette and balance it in the tray, then gather his bounty and deposit it in a canvas sack on the floor.

Three cigarettes later, he will lift the rabbit from his lap and take it to its hutch in the kitchen gardens. Then he will return, a new rabbit, large and heavy and fluffy in his arms. When the sack is full, Charles will bring out his cards—Jean knows this is what they are called because he asked and Charles said, Have a go. The cards are like brushes but wider and flatter with short wooden handles and tiny metal teeth. Charles will place the fur along the teeth and press the cards together, brushing in opposite directions. When Jean did it, the sound made his gums hurt. Once the wool has been carded, it can be spun. This Charles does in private, however, because the spinning wheel is in his room, and he got it from his mother, and he doesn't want the boys to fuck it up.

Today he has a rabbit in class—they moult more in the summer—and, as he speaks, his hand swipes along its back.

Charles's classroom is upstairs in what would have formerly been the salon. There are no desks, chalkboard, or cane. Instead the walls are covered, floor to ceiling, in art—bowls of fruit, small dogs, a family portrait, and even some newer works, abstract shapes and coloured squares. At one end of the room there is a small, round wooden table that fits five students. This is where Tom now sits with Hugo, Theo, Percy, and Samuel. Jean is in one of the padded window seats. No one has sat next to him—they rarely do—so he has the luxury of stretching his legs along its length. Colin lies belly down on the oriental rug, stabbing the stretch of floorboards between rug and wall with a knife. Charles sits in one of the low, corduroy armchairs on the other side of the room by the fireplace and the chaise longue. He produces a pair of scissors and teases them along the rabbit's body. From Jean's viewpoint he cannot see the animal's face, but he notices an ear twitch.

Charles has told Jean that sometimes it is necessary to trim the fur. As Charles cuts now, mounds of fluffy white fall to the floor. These are called clouds. Outside the sky is blue and clear. The sun filtering through the large oak makes patterns in the classroom, across Charles's face, the frozen rabbit.

Dappled, anyone? Charles says.

The boys have their faces on the table. Samuel, who is short with ginger hair, is gently snoring. Charles raps the scissors against the wide, stone fireplace, and he jolts up. The rabbit, too, jumps from Charles's lap and hops under a side table.

Nice of you to join us, Samuel, Charles says. We were just talking about the meaning of the word *dappled*. Any ideas?

The bruise from where Jean punched Samuel last week has faded to yellow.

Neat?

Aha! Charles stands, white fur cascading from his lap. A classic homophonic confusion. You're thinking of *dapper*. Lovely.

The other strange thing about Charles is the way he talks to students. Like when he told Jean he was smart and it didn't matter that he was dyslexic. In fact, Charles says Jean could do really brilliantly on the exam, really quite brilliantly. Jean didn't know what to say when Charles told him that so he said nothing. But he has held on to the knowledge delicately and with anticipation, like a bun fresh from the oven, ever since.

Dappled is the opposite, Charles says now.

The boys are supposed to write this stuff down, but most exercise books are pitifully empty. Jean watches as Tom rips out a sheet of paper and begins folding. Hugo is carving something into the table, Theo is methodically pulling all the stuffing out of a chair seat, while Colin is trying to lure the rabbit from its hiding place with a bit of old bread. Charles does not notice the group's ennui; or he doesn't care. His classes are often chaotic and yet there is a sense, for the most part, that the boys respect—or is it fear?—him. That, even if it is not in the classroom, he can teach them something. Charles has hitched around America, picked tobacco in Canada, and followed the Silk Road to Afghanistan. Late at night, after David has gone to bed, Charles will tell the boys about the colours of LSD, the smell of poppy-seed tea, and the bitter, earthy taste of magic mushrooms. Only after David has gone to bed, of course. Drugs are strictly forbidden.

Today Charles is wearing a striped shirt and linen shorts. His trademark glasses. Some of the rabbit fur has stuck to his legs.

Couple-colour, brinded cow, rose-moles on fish, he says. Or think of it this way, Matron's excuse of a car—

Sexy little banger!

Your hole-ridden pumps, Colin. As Charles steps over him, he gives the boy a gentle kick in the arse. But you like them, right? Other examples, things that aren't perfect.

Earlier that day, Tom and Jean had caught a fish; the slick body wriggling in Tom's hands. The way its skin puckered, the marks on its back. A brown trout, Tom told him. You could tell because it looked like a leopard.

Millie's knickers!

Millie's knickers, Charles repeats gleefully. Why do we love them?

Tom is still bent over his book, hands moving. He has been growing out his hair and it is past his ears. But it is uneven and a tuft at the back is longer than the rest. Jean catches Charles's eye and flushes. Did Charles see him staring at Tom?

Jean! Charles points the scissors at him. Why might Hopkins celebrate imperfections?

Because—images of reeds and water and spots, the dots on the fish's slick body, flick across Jean's vision—Because those are the bits that make them, them.

Tom's tuft of hair.

Go on, Charles says.

Like a cow with patches is a cow.

The whole class is looking at him, Jean realises, in silence. Colin hops onto his knees and moos. Hugo chucks a pencil sharpener and Jean ducks.

Or something. Jean slumps farther into the window seat.

Yes, good, Jean.

Charles crosses the room, kicking Colin again; Colin falls and Charles mutters, Get up you stupid boy.

Take it as a metaphor, Charles says.

A paper plane sails into Jean's cheek. In it, the note: *Lake later comrade?* He folds the message once, twice, three times, and puts it in his mouth, chewing until the paper is a mushy paste. More planes dive around him.

Settling the rabbit back in his lap and resuming trimming it, Charles says, Gentlemen, this is for your benefit, not mine. Let's get this over with so we can all get out and enjoy the afternoon sunshine.

The boys at the table cheer and hammer the floor with their feet.

Yes, yes. We've established that Hopkins is pro imperfections. Why? *Praise Him*. When do we say that?

No one responds. Charles sighs.

What Hopkins says, *children*, is that imperfections are good because they are evidence of God. If beauty is inherently flawed, then—the scissors glint in the sun—does that make God flawed?

A fine thread, just like the Angora wool that Charles spins, spools from Jean.

Let's flip it. In a Christian world, humans are sinful, dirty things.

Snip, the scissors cut.

Perhaps it is precisely that, our capacity for sin, that makes us beautiful, Charles says, quieter now, so the class must strain to hear. What do you like the most? What feels really good?

Charles looks at the boys, scissors hovering, eyes coloured purple by the lenses of his glasses.

It's probably bad. In a Christian world it's probably terrible.

Nervous sniggers from the class. The thread tugs at Jean from somewhere below his rectum through his stomach. He strains against it but feels himself moving, imperceptibly, forward and upward, toward the ceiling. Woodchips have gathered where Colin has been cutting up the floor.

But it's probably human, Charles says, his voice louder now. Hopkins was a very conflicted man. He engaged in this heightened, erotic relationship—

And Jean is no longer in the classroom. He is ten and sitting in the kitchen of Mick Caro, the musician who lives around the corner. Jean sits on a high stool at the breakfast bar, which is chrome, reflecting the grey of outside. Micky opens the massive silver fridge that is built into the cabinets. Unlike Jean's kitchen, Micky's is all continuous lines and gleaming objects. Micky retrieves a bottle of milk, pours Jean a glass, and places it in front of him. Jean is too old for milk these days, but he does not say that to Micky. It is 1969 and Micky moved into the house a few streets over only a couple of months ago. He is an *almost* famous singer and even though he must be close to forty, he is Jean's friend (maybe even his *best* friend—didn't he tell Jean to call him Micky, not Mick?).

Every day, when Micky isn't recording his new album, Jean goes over, and every day, Micky gives him milk and biscuits. The white liquid reaches the very lip of the glass, threatening to spill so Jean must lap it up like a cat. The room is filled with the strong scent of incense. "Suzanne" by Leonard Cohen plays softly on the radio. Rain flecks the wide, flat glass doors that cover the length of one wall looking out to the garden. The chrome countertop against which Micky rests, watching Jean, is dull in the muted light, revealing its scratches.

Don't stop, Micky says, when, after Jean has lapped an adequate amount, he attempts to pick up the glass. You look funny like that.

As the liquid disappears, Jean leans farther into the glass, pressing his mouth against the rim, slurping the milk until his tongue can no longer reach but flails, naked and dripping with saliva in the empty space. There is a sore mark around Jean's mouth where the glass has made an imprint. Micky takes the empty glass, fills it to the top, places it in front of Jean. His eyes crinkle. Again.

And somewhere else, Charles is still talking about love and sin and sex and Hopkins who was really a—

Faggot.

A voice that is not Charles's rings out clear and sharp in the classroom, snapping the thread from Jean's stomach so he lands, heavy, back in his seat. Hugo is smiling and frowning at the same time, pleased with himself.

The class erupts. Colin whacks his knife against the wall, Theo stands on a chair, Tom thumps the table, while Hugo remains still, breathing heavily, his lips parted and slightly wet, as they chant: Faggot, faggot.

Charles says nothing but colour creeps into his cheeks. Then: Alright. Louder still: Alright!

The noise peters out until it is just Hugo, and then nothing but embarrassed snorts. Whispers that radiate.

Faggot, Charles says. *Faggot*. Know where the word comes from Hugo?

Hugo giggles.

It is a bundle of sticks for firewood, something servants would have gathered when this house was first built. At some point it was used to describe an old woman, the very same woman who collected said sticks. We could, Charles says, moving his hand to the rabbit's bottom, lifting gently, and trimming the fine fur around its anus, Call Matron a faggot. It is also chopped liver, which, by the way, is delicious with Bordeaux, and in Yiddish *faygele* means little bird.

It may be Jean's imagination, but it seems as if Charles's eyes flick toward him as he says *Yiddish*. And does Tom turn around?

None of this helps us, though, Charles looks at Hugo. Does it?

Hugo's eyes, now dull and unfocused, drift somewhere above Charles's head.

Most likely, Charles says, Is that the word in the way you, Hugo, just used it, comes from the nasty things boys force each other to do at boarding school.

Hugo meets Charles's gaze. The silence feels very loud. The muscles in Hugo's face twitch. But he must see the scissors in Charles's hand too: how Charles has shifted, brandishing them like a knife.

But, Charles says, his voice suddenly lighter, We can discuss the etymology after class if you like. Let's not waste any more of anyone else's time.

Sweat stains have pooled under Hugo's armpits. He is wearing a grubby white T-shirt and torn jeans. His hair is long and brown and sticks to his wide, pink forehead. He is not the tallest boy in the school but he is one of the strongest, as is clear whenever he fights. Hugo has been at Compton Manor since he was small; his parents won't have him home even during the holidays.

Poetry is like that, Charles says. Several strands of thought, multiple images, can coexist in the same space, coming to the surface at different points.

The boys resume their small rebellions; Colin on the floor, cutting up the boards, and Tom drawing on the face of a sleeping Samuel. But Jean's heart hammers; he closes his eyes and watches the sunspots behind his lids multiply and divide.

Before Plato and Socrates, there were Byron and Tiny, Charles Burrows' first iteration of rabbits. Byron was an English Angora and Tiny was a Giant. Tiny stopped eating, becoming thinner and thinner. At first Charles thought it was protein deficiency and drove to town to buy special pellets. Then he thought it was the water supply and purchased bottles of mineral water. But still Tiny refused any food or water. One day, as Charles was cleaning the cage, Tiny jumped on Byron, gnawing his throat. Charles was seen sprinting across the lawn, Byron gripped between his hands, blood seeping down his arms. Byron was buried by the statue of Aphrodite on the main lawn. Later, Tiny died too.

Jean opens his eyes; the classroom is mostly in shadow now. Hugo mimes a gun, aims at Jean's head, fires. Charles brushes his legs, tanned skin emerging from beneath white hair. When Charles got new rabbits, Jean asked him if he was scared to keep them in the same hutch. It's fine, Charles said. One of them is a doe.

It is only male rabbits who attack each other when confined in the same space.

Are you going to eat that? Samuel asks.

Cook has been experimenting with curry again. A puddle of red sauce with a few lone chickpeas sits next to a ball of rice. Jean pushes his plate toward Samuel. At home, Rosa makes lamb chops; red slabs sizzling under the grill, covered in rosemary and garlic and dripping fat. Potato fondant cooked in the depths of butter. Or vegetables, freshly cut and raw. Pepper, cucumber, endive.

When Jean was younger, he would follow her around the kitchen, and she would explain what she was doing. How it was important to dice the onions, carrots, and celery this small; how with this base you could cook almost anything. Soup, sauce, casserole. She would give him jobs, his little fingers grappling with the pea pod, fumbling to catch the green pearls that popped out. Or plucking the stalks from blackcurrants, his mouth stained an incriminating purple, Rosa's too, baring their teeth at each other and pretending to be vampires. Him screeching with glee, her picking him up and nuzzling her nose against his. He used to love cooking with Rosa. The peace that would settle in the room as they concentrated. That was something. How they could be silent together, working side by side. The joy of the thing they made.

She certainly wasn't silent these days, and often he found himself too nauseous to eat.

But what he would give for a moist chicken thigh now, some crispy skin. Or—he sinks his spoon into the soft sponge of his pudding, feels the scalding custard burn the roof of his mouth—her apricot tart, jewels of orange in a pool of light crème pat.

I love spotted dick, Samuel says.

Despite their altercation the other day, Samuel sits with Jean at mealtimes. He also lets Jean copy his homework. Samuel is short and skinny and seems to have an endless appetite. The yellow around his eye has a tinge of green to it. Jean feels a pang of guilt and passes his pudding bowl. He's not hungry. His stomach drops when he remembers later, and the lake. He wonders if he should ask the kitchen for scraps. He imagines Tom's face when he arrives, bait in hand.

So? Samuel says, his face enquiring, two spots of yellow at the corners of his mouth.

What?

Samuel frowns at the last of his pudding as if the answer might be there. Then he scoops it up and puts it in his mouth with relish.

Do you still want my physics? You can have it before the film.

Outside the sun is low and beams of syrupy light cut into the room through the lattice windows. The dining hall forms the centre of the school and is what David calls its *jewel*. Jean has heard him describe it to prospective parents, explaining that this was once where the original owners would hold large hunting balls. Because this was in the seventeenth century, the ceilings are low. But rather than make the space feel cramped, it imbues it with an intimate grandeur. The walls are wood-panelled, hung with tapestries and paintings of the family (including the current owner, Sir Stephen Bolton). At one end is the fireplace, practically a room itself, which is lit on special occasions. The ceiling, the wooden walls and floor amplify and dampen the acoustics of the room, so that the noise of the boys—someone lobs a roll across the hall, someone else yells—comes to Jean as if through a filter, distorted.

Across the long dark tables, he can see Tom in the middle of a group, gesturing. His hands are delicate with long fingers like those of a piano player. As Tom speaks, his eyes flick to Jean's.

Not going, Jean says.

To the film? Samuel says. Why? Then, when Jean doesn't respond: Why'd you do that?

Jean follows Samuel's gaze to where his own hand is pinching the inside of his arm. He hadn't even noticed. It is something he did as a child. His teachers used to question him about the bruises that lined his inner right arm—was everything OK at home, did his mother hurt him?—until they noticed how often he gripped his flesh. The lady doctor with glasses asked him about it too. Why did he want to hurt himself? Rosa went mad if she caught him at it. Truthfully, he has never known why he does it, and one day he stopped. He hasn't done it for years, not until recently, until Tom.

He forces himself to fold his hands in his lap. Laughter from Tom's table makes the hairs on his neck stand up. Samuel is talking about the film, how it was shot somewhere in the desert and how the actress is held captive by some evil natives. Samuel pauses, retrieves his inhaler, and takes a hit. She's meant, he whispers between breaths, To be naked!

The dinner hall is filling with the sound of cutlery and chairs, boys on the move. And Samuel is still talking about the woman in the film, and if you can see her breasts, and if she will ride a motorcycle, and if there will be horses. Once Jean's heart is beating at a normal rate again, he pushes his chair back, stands up, and exits, leaving a bemused Samuel alone. Jean is careful to avoid looking in Tom's direction; he doesn't want to give them, himself, away. He goes straight to his room, changes into his boots, packs his knife and cough drops tin in his rucksack and heads out. It is only when he is halfway across the field that he realises he forgot to ask for bait. No matter, Tom is sure to bring some.

In their usual spot at the side of the lake, he stretches out on a log in the last of the evening sun. He is early but that doesn't matter. Was Tom saying something with his eyes earlier, when he looked at Jean from across the hall? A secret code that only they know. The sun warms Jean's lids, and he replays the interaction over and over, each time a new message shooting from Tom. Like some kind of cordless telephone without the sound. It would have been nice if, earlier, he could have turned down Rosa's voice on the telephone.

Things really shifted between them when Jean went to Compton Manor. Things had always been tricky, yes, but after he left for school, a new layer of difficulty cloaked them. He had never really forgiven her for sending him here; but now, he hated going home. Suddenly faced with her after months away, he found her idiosyncrasies unbearable. It occurs to him now that she might have the same experience with him. Was that why, when he was back at Easter, things were especially bad?

She had insisted on making an elaborate dinner. The sight of her: her hair awry, jeans slung low on her hips, pressing a green and fragrant butter between the chicken's skin and flesh. She interrogated him, asking him question after question, becoming more manic the less he spoke. He'd been unable to eat in the end, and Rosa, finishing her second bottle of merlot, had dumped the chicken dramatically into the bin, steam rising from the black bin liner.

What will she be doing now? Jean wonders, head resting against the log's hard surface. Sitting on the sagging brown velvet sofa in the living room, the glare of the box her only light, the Ricard ashtray full of butts, washing piled in the corner by the machine, the sink stacked with dirty dishes? Or will she be in her studio—the room that sits above the kitchen and runs the length of the house, so she gets light from both sides—lemons, jug, and bowl arranged before her, half-finished painting perched on the easel, staring in fixed concentration that she will maintain until the dustmen come at dawn? Or will she have called Dinah, her best friend, colleague, kind of family, who spends as much time at their house as her own; the two of them sitting in the kitchen, a bottle between them, Rosa moaning about her son? Will she be with one of her students, snaked in the sheets upstairs.

Despite himself, and contrary to what Rosa believes, Jean does worry. He worries what people say about her, what they think. He worries she is lonely.

But it is not his problem. He shakes away these thoughts and tries to put himself back to half an hour ago when he was looking at Tom and Tom was looking at him. But where is Tom? He sits up. The sun is touching the fields, making the tall grass taller, setting the world ablaze. He squints, looking at the hill Tom should crest any minute now. But Tom does not appear and the deep orange sun sinks lower, like a coin in a slot machine, until it has disappeared below the horizon. The world is flat again, the shadows dissipating into a blanket of lilac. Jean sits on the log and waits. He sits there while lilac turns to purple, purple to deep navy. Eventually, when the first stars appear, he moves, stiff and aching, and walks back to school. It is dark, the moon a sliver in the sky. As he moves through the inky black, he notices he has no shadow, and he wonders if Tom still wants to go to China.

Jean can hear the elevated music of the end credits emanating from the common room. Boys pour out the door, talking and shoving, and Jean stands to one side to let them pass. He sees Samuel in deep discussion with another boy, making circular motions with his hands. Tom appears with someone else, Gus or Harry, Jean can't remember his name. Jean wills Tom to turn and see him, but then Gus or Harry says something and Tom tips his head back in laughter, throws his arm around Gus or Harry and saunters away.

III

THE FIRST TIME IT HAPPENS, JEAN AND TOM ARE BY THE LAKE. It is three days after the film night.

In the morning, Jean wakes before sunrise and goes outside to meditate. He settles himself on the grass, the damp seeping through his shorts and onto his bare skin.

Years ago, when Jean was eleven, he arranged himself just so in the heat of Micky's kitchen. Micky showed Jean how to place his left hand in his right, thumbs touching: This is the cosmic mudra, he said, The whole of the universe in your hands, my dude. Then he told Jean to slow his breathing, to focus on the first moment air touched lips. Just that, nothing else. Jean tried, but he couldn't concentrate. It was summer and, before the meditation, Micky had stripped to his underwear. Jean had not seen a man so bare before (there was a camp leader in Wales; and dads on holiday beaches, but those were quick, unsubstantial flashes in public) and he was shocked. Micky's confidence had occluded Jean's doubt, however, so that when Micky tapped the floor in front of him, Jean took off his own vest and shorts. But sitting in front of Micky, strong, manly, while Jean was only in his flimsy Y-fronts, he could not concentrate. His legs ached, his nose itched, the floor was making him sweat, and in his mind, the shape of Micky's domed biceps rotated.

As dawn spreads over the Sussex Downs now, Jean is distracted again. The wet sticks the fabric of his shorts to his buttocks and the cold makes him shiver. He should have brought a jumper, but he tries to put that out of his mind. Bruce Lee would tell him the material world is a distraction; jumper or no jumper, it doesn't matter. The first rays of sunlight skim across the meadow and glance off his knees and chest.

At some point, though, he stopped fidgeting in Micky's kitchen. He focused on the heat that warmed his legs, the feeling of his breath entering and leaving him. Slowly, thoughts of Micky dissipated, as did thoughts about himself, becoming translucent, weightless things. Sound amplified—the sharp bang of a backfired engine, the staggered trail of piano scales—and quietened. The room expanded and contracted and then fell away completely. There was only his breath left, in and out, like a leaf blowing in the wind. And so it happens again, now, as he clears his head, focusing on the first rays on his skin, the wind across his face, the grass tickling his feet; as he counts—one, two, three, four—as he focuses on when air becomes breath, light becomes dark, something nothing; as he relaxes his limbs, letting their weight drop down toward, into, and through the ground; so Jean lifts upward, evaporating from his body like steam. The universe in Jean's hands explodes, Jean becomes nothing, and everything disappears.

In this nonplace of nonexistence, Jean, or non-Jean, hovers. He is a current in the air, a single bright ray, a soft murmur. It is as if the world, its forms and shapes, has dissolved into itself. Tom, Micky, homework, Rosa, those heavy, dense things become nothing more than the dew that rises around him, filling a shape that glows white. A white space of indistinguishable structure, a rectangle inside him that opens out and fills up.

After, Jean goes to the farm.

He is first there and spends some time checking the fences around the chicken coop. Foxes are always a problem. Jean admires how they always find new and different ways of getting in. He reattaches some loose chicken wire and hammers in a peg. Sometimes, the foxes have help. A boy left the coop door ajar once and the next day they found only a few feathers and some streaks of blood. What amazes Jean is how silently it happened. All those bodies, packed tightly together in one room, slaughtered. He thinks, briefly, of people packed together, falling down one by one as poisonous gas fills the space. He read somewhere that no one screamed. Jean admires the foxes but he hates them a little bit as well.

Inside, the coop is warm and dry. The sounds of soft clucking and the rustle of feathers. Jean lifts one bird from her perch; her head jerks silently left and right. Her legs stretch out to meet the floor and she struts into the open air. He is reminded of being nine and opening Rosa's underwear drawer; the noise the nylons made as he rifled through them, how each one stretched outward, seemingly never-ending, like ribbons from a magician's hat. Soft to the touch.

He feeds the chickens, watching as they jostle each other at the trough, like old women at the market. He refills their water and collects the eggs, placing them in his basket gently, careful not to crack them. Next, he cleans out the coop, adding the dirty straw to the compost round the back. Then he fills the coop again, making sure each chicken has the same level of bedding. As he works, he talks. How are we today, missy? Don't you have a pretty coat on you. Feeling shy?

By the time he is done, the sun is bright and he has a light sweat. He drops off the fresh eggs at the kitchen, goes to the dormitory to change, and to the main hall for breakfast.

He has been struggling to eat the last few days—ever since Tom did not show—but this morning he has two boiled eggs, dipping his toast into the perfect liquid-gold centre.

As he is finishing, Tom comes up to him. The top of Tom's nose is burnt pink and starting to blister, and there is gummy sleep in the corners of his eyes. Jean's stomach drops. He wishes he hadn't eaten two eggs. Jean hasn't asked Tom why he did not show the other night and Tom hasn't said anything. Jean has the sensation that Tom has been avoiding him. This is how it goes. In nursery when Peter stopped talking to him and in primary school when Simon pushed him over on the playground. Scraped knees on gravel. Jean doesn't pretend to understand how friendships work. He assumed Tom had changed his mind and that was that. He is surprised, then, to find Tom standing before him. Just when he got his appetite back.

The heat of the day has not yet descended on the Downs and Jean's arms pimple with the breeze. Tom pauses and points to the sky where the outline of a bird circles. Hawk? Jean wonders aloud. No, Tom says. Buzzard.

The grass tickles their shins as they lope across the meadow. At the lake, the path is clearer, the mud hard and dehydrated from the sun. On one side stiff reeds bristle. Jean can hear the movements of animals between the stalks—voles, water rats, frogs. The meadow disappears behind them in a curl of pale green as they turn toward the woods. The shadows make the air cooler and damp. Jean has the feeling of stepping into another world. Here, the path is less clear, and they must fight through the undergrowth, lifting their legs over the bracken and dipping under low-hanging branches.

A thorn snags Jean's shorts and he is pulled backward. Once he has extricated himself, Tom has disappeared. Jean has not been to this side of the lake before, and he moves slowly. Nettles sting; he almost trips on a root. Was this Tom's plan: lead him here and leave him, stuck among the weeds? Or worse? The wheelchair that was found submerged in the lake; the buzzard that tipped and fell from the sky, outstretched claws ready to snatch its prey. But then he pushes through a wall of green and he is in open space and Tom is there, grinning.

The clearing sits between the woods and the lake. Trees and foliage line the back of it; at the other end stands a willow, its wide, white trunk mottled and its curved limbs, heavy with feathery leaves, bent toward the water, creating a screen and protecting the boys from view.

I found it last year, Tom says. No one else knows about it.

Tom has two rods and some scraps from the kitchen. He helps Jean fasten the meat to the hook—It would be better if we had live ones, but this'll do—and cast the line. There is a log by the edge of the lake that Tom positioned the last time he was here, and that works perfectly as a balance for the rods.

We'd either need to go through Russia or through Iran, Tom says.

Jean takes his tin out and begins to roll.

Probably we want to do Russia. Less chance of being killed, Tom continues.

Jean licks the paper and folds.

But then again, the Russians are crazy bastards.

Jean taps the joint so it settles, lights it, and passes it to Tom, who takes a long hit.

The Trans-Siberian Railway, Tom exhales. Sounds good, doesn't it?

Yeah. The weed and something else move through Jean.

Makes me think of tigers for some reason. Is that stupid? That's stupid.

Jean leans on his elbows. He didn't expect this. He didn't think Tom still wanted to go to China; he definitely didn't expect him to look up the route. Jean has spent time studying the maps in the library, tracing the journey from Moscow down through Kirov, Perm, Ekaterinburg, Omsk, Novosibirsk. Cities that sit heavy on his tongue, that took him three, four, five attempts to pronounce. Cities that sound like codes. Escape routes.

One is on a lake, Jean says.

The tenth stop, Irkutsk, sits at the mouth of the river Irkut, which flows from Lake Baikal. It is the deepest lake in the world. The oldest, too, at thirty million years. Imagine what lingers in its depths; creatures from the past who know only darkness.

It freezes in winter. You can walk on it.

Tom flicks an ant from his arm. We don't want to go in winter.

No.

Miles and miles of transparent floor. Time stopped, mid-flow.

We'll stop, though, Tom says.

Yeah.

Do some fishing.

Irkutsk.

What?

Irkutsk, Jean tries again. That's the city.

Like the river?

You know it?

My dad has these maps. Rivers, lakes, seas. Tom kicks a log to the side as he says, He made us learn them all. He was a right prick about it.

Jean takes a long drag. He has only met his own father once. He was young and the contours of the memory are blurred, but he recalls a tall man with blond hair. Jean did something that angered him and embarrassed Rosa and, after that, his father left. Jean did not see him again. He does not know his name; he does not know what he does or where he lives or if he is still alive. When he was younger, Jean asked Rosa these questions but she spoke about his father vaguely—he was just around, he played the piano, he lived in the country—and when Jean pressed the point, Rosa got upset, worrying the edge of her lip and saying, Who gives a fuck about men? They're weak.

Bit of a prick in general, Tom says now.

Jean passes back the joint. When he was little, he pretended his father was an astronaut. His father was a spy. A travelling salesman. A sailor. A pirate. A Tibetan monk who had taken a vow of silence, renouncing all humanity. Outrageous stories that answered the questions Rosa could not, would not. That explained why he never got a birthday card or Christmas card. When he was older, he considered searching for his father, but he didn't have anything to go on. Rosa had given him a photograph, which Jean kept in a shoebox under his bed until he was eleven. He happened to be flicking through one of her magazines and stopped at a series of vintage photographs of a just deceased American politician. At first, he was excited. *That* was his father. Then he realised the opposite was true: Rosa had simply cut out the picture. Something shifted for Jean then. He tossed the picture into the bin. His father is nothing; an air bubble trapped somewhere below his throat. Tom's father may be a prick but at least he is there.

Irkutsk, Jean says. It's where—you know when they talk about sending people to Siberia?

No.

That's where they sent them. If you pissed off the government, they sent you to this shit hole.

Jean takes another hit on the joint. In the shade of the willow, it is cool, and Jean shivers. Tom looks at him out of one eye, the other closed against the glare from the lake.

The Paris of Siberia, Jean says.

How do you know this shit? Tom spreads himself on the ground next to Jean.

Jean imagines a tiny Eiffel Tower in the middle of a snow-covered, wind-lashed plain. He read about it in the library when tracing the route to China. Jean has always known things of no consequence; yet he seems unable to retain what his teachers tell him. This, the lady doctor with the glasses told him, is on account of his dyslexia; others say he is stupid. His brain is filled with scrolls of random facts, pictures of faraway places, song lyrics. Things he is quite sure will be useless in his upcoming O-levels.

Irkut means spinning, he says.

Spinning?

Yeah. Spinning.

The river spinning faster and faster away from its source and toward something larger. Because that is the beautiful thing about water. How it moves in all directions at once and how it has a single route. Bruce Lee.

Irkutsk, Tom says and sniggers.

Irkutsk? Jean repeats and Tom cracks up.

Irkuuutsk.

Irku*tsk*.

Jean smiles and says the word again, trying out different emphases. Tom is right. The word—awkward in their English mouths—is funny. A wave of hilarity washes over them as the high hits like a freight train. It's hard to explain why, but the word is so funny they can barely breathe. Tom grips Jean's arm to steady himself but Jean is floppy, and they fall onto their backs, the effort needed to be upright too much. Irkutsk, Irkutsk, Irkutsk, Irkutsk. Was anything ever so funny?

They gasp for breath, Irkutsk leaving them in whispers. They are side by side, the joint forgotten somewhere on the grass. Above them the light sparkles in the gaps between the willow leaves, now thick, now thin, now blinding, now blank. Jean has forgotten about his father; the only thing that matters is being here with Tom, the grass beneath them.

Irkutsk, Jean shouts in a fake Russian accent and Tom cracks up again. He rolls over and as he does so, his chest lands heavy on Jean's tricep, his stomach on Jean's forearm and something else, hard and firm, presses into Jean's hand. Tom is still giggling, face down. His body convulses with the last shudders of laughter and with every movement he presses his erection into Jean's hand. Jean has stopped laughing. He tries to breathe evenly but he can feel his own erection rising.

A gust of wind makes the leaves clap together and shakes yellow, dried leaves onto them. Tom is breathing shallow, fast. This sound mixes with the arhythmic lapping of water and the rustling branches. So, too, the frantic movements of insects by Jean's ears overlay the roar of a plane in the sky. As if the world has flattened, as if Jean is experiencing some deep interconnectedness between all living things. Tom could imagine that Jean's arm is a branch, or part of the forest floor. Jean could curl his fingers around Tom. It would be easy. He keeps his palm as flat and still as possible, letting Tom press himself harder into it. But then Tom is up, whipping round to the lake.

Fuck. How much did you put in that?

Jean turns to the woods, tucking his semi into his waistband. He massages his arm. The pain in his elbow is sharp and insistent. He might have twinged something.

I blacked out just then, Tom says.

Jean waits until his voice will be at a safe pitch, then he says: Me too.

Fuck. That was like a seriously heavy amount.

Yeah.

That shit is lethal.

The bait has been eaten from the rods without the boys noticing. Tom fumbles for more, reattaching it.

You trying to fuck me up, Blondie?

As Tom pierces a piece of old chicken onto the hook, his hands shake and the morsel drops to the ground.

Stop fucking staring.

Jean tries counting to nine, but the numbers get mixed up in his head. He contemplates ramming Tom into the lake but instead he strikes a match and takes a long drag on the joint.

No way, Tom says when Jean extends it toward him.

Jean reflects on some of the things he could call Tom: chicken boy, chicken fillet, plain old chicken, and smiles to himself. King Cock.

Finally, Tom re-hooks the bait, but he can't cast the line. He howls and throws the rod into the shallows.

Give me that. Tom says, taking several short drags and holding them in his chest.

There is a bald patch of earth where Jean has ripped up the grass.

The second time it happens they are in the meadow. It is two days later. The sun is directly above them. It is lunchtime. While the others were still eating in the hall, Tom and Jean slipped out. Butterflies flit between the red shock of the bow-lipped poppies, and the electric-blue cornflowers. Tom is talking about fishing.

My pa took us every morning. Down to the lake.

Jean has his eyes closed and Tom's voice is soft and low, soothing.

He taught us the whipping method, Tom says.

Jean opens one eye to watch Tom demonstrate.

You hold the rod like this, one hand here, and one hand down here. And you imagine there's a dog. And you whip it.

Tom's wrist, pale and strong, angles forward and back. Tom's forearm, how the muscles tense, how it hinges at the elbow. To be that dog, whipped by Tom.

Right, Jean says.

Fishing is like praying my pa says. You do it every day.

Jean closes his eyes; he smiles. The heat presses down on his lids.

What? Tom says.

Didn't realise you were such a good Christian.

Shut up, Tom says. Anyway, Jesus was a fisherman.

Jean laughs at that.

What'll we catch in Siberia? Tom says, flopping next to Jean. Something tickles Jean's forearm, and he opens his eyes, half expecting to find Tom poised above him. But it is just a butterfly, her pale green wings the same colour as the parched grass.

Arctic grayling, Jean says.

Grayling?

Jean doesn't tell Tom that he has been waiting for this question. That, since the last time by the lake, he has gone back to the library, and he has found a book on *Fishing Through the World*. He lifts a finger to the butterfly, and she tentatively climbs toward it.

They're part of the salmon family, Jean says.

I know.

They have them in Canada and Alaska. Missouri too.

The butterfly rests on the pad of his finger, one leg sliding under his nail. Tom is staring at him.

I'm surprised, Blondie. We'll make a fisherman of you yet.

Anywhere on the Arctic drainages, Jean says. That's why they're called arctic grayling.

You are so full of shit.

Call me Jesus, Jean says. The butterfly lifts up and away. Jean lies back, closes his eyes.

Jesus could actually fish, Tom says. Then: Fuck it's hot.

Jean hears rather than sees Tom take off his T-shirt. Tom is pale, unlike Jean whose skin goes dark in the sun and whose hair lightens almost to white. Jean imagines Tom's smooth, white torso, bare to the sun's rays. If he opens his eyes, he will be able to see the veins under Tom's skin, a network of green and blue that reminds Jean of fish, that makes Tom a merman. A bead of sweat slides down Jean's armpit.

George is coming down in a few weeks, Tom says.

The illustrious, famous, fantastic brother George. The George that Tom speaks about with both bitterness and admiration, who will take over the business, who already has a degree in land economy, who is a Blues rugby player. Jean doesn't know what either of those things are, but Tom told him with such reverence that Jean doesn't feel he can ask.

Cool, Jean says, but really, he doesn't want George to come down. Men like George usually hate Jean.

We can go fishing. I warn you, though, he's more fly than bait.

Jean does not know what that means. He will have to go back to the library. He takes off his own T-shirt, turning away from Tom as he does so. When he was little, Rosa made him take swimming lessons. He spent the bus journey there in a state of quiet dread: the humid, chlorinated air that made his eyes sting and his clothes damp; the wild, hysterical cries that echoed off the domed ceiling; and, worst of all, the tight, noisy changing rooms, where who-should-know-whose strange bottom or breast would come bobbing into view. By the time Jean reached the water's edge, he was desperate, ineffectually covering his body with his skinny arms. He couldn't explain to Rosa why it was impossible for him to go into the water: that he felt, standing on the side, the other children torpedoing around him, both exposed and trapped. But, he realises, he wants that now—to be exposed and trapped—with Tom.

Jean lies back, careful to place his arm out—near Tom but not touching—and it happens almost immediately. Tom yawns with exaggerated movements, then rolls over. He moves, imperceptibly, forward and backward, and Jean curls his fingers, imperceptibly, so they press into the fabric of Tom's shorts.

Jean's eyes are closed; he imagines Tom's are too. Tom's pale back toward the sun. It will be turning pink like a ripening strawberry.

Tom's hand, limp and passive, lands on Jean's thigh, just below his groin. Inches.

When Jean refused to get into the swimming pool, Rosa marched him through the atrium and into the changing room. There, she thrust him down on the bench, saying what a fucking waste of money that was. She was wearing men's shorts and an oversized denim shirt. Her large silver hoops and bangles shook as she snapped the goggles from his head, the armbands from his shoulders and, in front of everyone, tugged his Speedos to the floor. It is this that comes back to him now, as Tom's hand rests on his inner thigh: the feeling of Rosa's rough hands on his body. Years later and she still doesn't knock on his bedroom door before entering. If he should be indecent, she will laugh and tell him not to be such a drama queen; the last time they were on holiday, she even slid her finger into the waistband of his shorts, pulling out the tucked drawstrings. On the nights she climbs into his bed, Jean is aware how thin the cotton of her nightdress is.

As a feeling of wrongness creeps over Jean, he flinches. At this slight movement, Tom retracts his hand, rolls away.

It will be good, Tom says, hoarse, When George comes.

Yeah, Jean says.

We should be careful. If they catch us then—Tom makes a cutthroat motion with one hand, the joint in the other.

Jean says nothing. He cannot believe Tom is speaking so openly.

Have you got a good hiding place? Tom says.

What?

Tom gestures with the joint to Jean's tin.

You know how Davey feels about drugs.

Oh. You mean the grass.

Yeah, Tom says, taking another drag, looking Jean in the eye. I mean the grass.

I keep it in a trunk under the bed.

Don't.

OK.

And don't come up to me in school or anything.

Tom winks and Jean feels sick, a sickness that comes from both fear and excitement.

The third time it happens, it is night. They are smoking before bed. It is a new moon, which means the sky is dark, which means she will appear again tomorrow.

They don't talk. It is late and it has been a long day.

After the joint, they both lie back. Jean knows what will happen and he isn't nervous. Jean extends his hand and Tom rolls onto it. Tom's arm falls across Jean's thigh. Tom is moving, really thrusting, and Jean is gripping, trying to get purchase through Tom's shorts, trying to find something that is firmer than material.

And it is dark, so dark that when Jean opens his eyes, he sees only blackness.

And there is the sound of Tom's breath and the calls of the crickets.

Those are the three times it happens. Then it stops. For more than a week, Jean goes every day to the spot in the clearing that Tom showed him, but Tom does not appear.

IV

COMPTON MANOR IS PLAYING A SCHOOL THAT COMES FROM somewhere near Brighton. The team arrives in an old, tatty bus, shoulders slouched, their kit ill-fitting. Eyes narrowed, they look at Compton Manor with suspicion, smoking cigarettes from the corners of their mouths. They have to be told two, three, four times before they amble onto the pitch.

Jean makes eye contact with one of them—a short boy with uneven facial hair—and adrenalin courses through him. During the match, the Brighton boys shout to one another and move with confidence, not afraid to get close, not afraid of touch, and the feeling tugs at Jean again. He does not want to be on the pitch—he's never been good at football or sport of any kind—but there is something in the Brighton players that he recognises. It reminds him of London. That breath before the fight.

Compton Manor plays a local team once a term, but Jean hasn't been to a game in a long time. When he first started at the school, he went to a couple matches, but he didn't like the way the other boys would grab him or ask him what team he supported or what position he played, exposing his lack of knowledge and training. Exposing him, once again, as some kind of freak who didn't have a father in his life to teach him crucial lessons like league tables and keepie-uppies and the offside rule.

Instead, Jean took the opportunity to get into the woods and spend some solid time undisturbed. He didn't mind being alone, he didn't mind that later he would have no idea what the boys were talking about. After a while, the others stopped trying to include him, knowing that if they pissed him off, which was likely, they would bear the brunt of his anger. Alone in the woods, he would practise his Wing Chun or go through his book of Zen philosophy. In Buddhist thought there is no place for competition. The ego is a distraction.

From somewhere behind him, someone shouts, Fucking foul. Ref, foul! as a Compton player takes a rolling tackle.

Supporters are spread on the hill behind the main house, the pitch nestled below them. It seems as if the whole school is here. Boys chant to the rhythm of "Let's go" by The Routers: Manor, Manor Boys, Manor Boys, Come, Let's go! Others hold a homemade banner that reads, "Compton: Loyal and True," in burgundy and white. Matron has made lemonade and hot dogs, and there is an air of conviviality and excitement that is infectious. Jean finds himself tense, crying out in dismay along with a chorus of others as the ref (an outsider who came with the local team) refuses to acknowledge the foul, telling the boy to get to his feet.

Another player wanders over and Jean realises with a sharp

intake of breath that it is Tom. The boy on the ground (Jean isn't sure of his name, someone from the younger years) grabs Tom's wrist and lets himself be hoisted up. Tom claps an arm around him. His white vest has turned grey with sweat and his shiny burgundy shorts are bunched around his groin, the polyester leaving little to the imagination.

Football lingo and statistics are not the only reason Jean doesn't watch the games. Tom may not have been aware of Jean's existence until recently, when he decided to break out of his boarding school habits and experiment with drugs, but Jean has been aware of Tom for some time. It was September 1974. Jean had just started at Compton Manor. This was when he still wanted to go home, when he used to beg Rosa to let him come back, when he would dream of London at night, the dark streets spotlit at intervals, the sour smell of pollution. The gigs that Kelly, the only good thing to have come out of his last school, used to take him to. When begging didn't work, he tried to run away. Then he tried punching walls. He didn't go to class. He didn't partake in extracurricular activities. Which was why he didn't know about the football team.

He was roaming the grounds looking for something to fuck up or burn when he heard the noise. There they were, eleven of them prancing around in shorts that barely covered their arses. Tom was shorter and slighter then. Still, there was something about the way he moved, graceful rather than aggressive, and that cowlick of hair, the way he smiled, embarrassed, when he fell, that wrenched something inside Jean.

Jean avoided watching the matches after that, avoided Tom in general, afraid of how much he wanted to be near him. To say that Jean thought Tom was a posh prick is not exactly true.

Rather, Tom seemed like such an impossibility, from a different solar system entirely, that the only way Jean could make sense of his longing was by rejecting it. When Tom came up to him a few weeks ago, Jean wasn't surprised; he was fucking terrified.

Now Tom wipes the sweat from his brow with his shirt, revealing the white, taut flesh of his stomach. The other boy is laughing at something Tom says, and Jean wants to know what is so funny. Tom grips the other boy's shoulder.

Jean would have missed this game, too, had Tom not come up to him, in school no less, while he was walking to class. He slapped Jean on the back and asked what was new, and Jean tried to ignore the burning sensation where Tom's hand had been. Tom had said not to talk to him at school, so Jean has kept to himself. Was this some kind of test? Then Jean found himself, despite his best efforts to remain calm, to dissolve his ego and be nothing but light and air, desperate to ask Tom where he had been all week. He pinched the inside of his arm to stop himself from telling Tom that he had waited, every night. As if Tom could read Jean's mind, he said:

Davey's been breaking my balls with practice.

And just like that, the block of ice between them melted away.

Anyway, Tom said as they approached the classroom, See you later?

When Jean looked over his shoulder, Tom was standing there, framed by the empty corridor.

Meanwhile the green shirts have possession of the ball. Tom sprints down the pitch. Jean watches the way his calf muscles tense, the breadth of his stride. He can't believe he has missed so many games, missed so many opportunities to see Tom soar down the pitch like a gazelle. Tom slide tackles a Brighton boy but he's too late, the player has already crossed the ball and now another runs forward, clipping the ball into the top right-hand corner of the net. The striker skids on his knees and his teammates pile on top of him. The crowd around Jean groans, and Tom is still on the ground staring in disbelief at the point where his foot almost made contact with the ball. He is beautiful, Jean thinks, even when he is disappointed.

Shit, Samuel says and takes a bite of his sandwich.

The Compton players huddle. From across the hill comes the scent of sausages, the boys' languorous chanting. The away side is pitifully empty, and the green shirts look blankly at the Compton fans. Jean is tight with the knowledge that Tom asked him to be here, that Tom wants him to watch. A bead of sweat slides down his neck and he leans back on his elbows. The Compton huddle breaks away and Tom turns to look up the hill, eyes searching. Could he be looking for Jean? Jean thinks, although he cannot be sure, that Tom clocks him. The electricity of recognition sizzles through him. Tom strides back to his position and it seems that as Tom moves, Jean moves too. Tom's body becomes Jean's; or rather, Jean holds Tom's body inside himself.

It is hot, and everyone is drenched in sweat. Jean can feel Tom's heart hammering in his chest. Feel his rabid desire. The whistle blows and their stomachs lift.

Terrible pass. He should have crossed it, Samuel says as a Compton player concedes the ball. Samuel was surprised when Jean followed him silently to the game. Surprised, and happy too. Samuel, who is ostracised for other reasons but who, unlike Jean, keenly wants to be a part of the gang—the Hugo, Tom, Theo, Percy gang—that dominates the school. Jean felt embarrassed for Samuel, for how happy he was that Jean was there, which is why he has endured Samuel's running commentary—even though it's fucking annoying—throughout the game.

The green shirts spread across the reds and Jean panics. Tom is having to run all over the pitch to help out. Jean can feel how tired he is; he wants to help him.

My dad took me to Chelsea–Crystal Palace, Samuel says.

Jean tries to recall what Bruce Lee said about telepathy, focusing on Tom. Jean may not know anything about football, but he knows something about movement. Poise and balance. As he exhales all the air from his lungs, something clicks. Jean wills Tom to hang back, and he does, bouncing from foot to foot.

Fucking savage, Samuel says, mouth full of crust, talking about the Chelsea match. All over each other before it's even started.

Suddenly the Brighton players seem to flounder. Passes don't meet their targets; the ball is kicked to the side. The green shirts are tired. Sweat sticks hair to spotty faces. Mouths open and gaping like fish out of water.

Samuel continues to prattle: One lad bottled another. I gave them something, too.

Into the space opened up by the green shirts, Jean guides Tom deftly, straining his legs so that, yes, he intercepts a lazy pass between two midfielders, and breaks away. He is alone, and the green shirts scramble backward. Jean shifts his weight and Tom tilts to the right, sweeping the ball back toward his own goal.

Nothing like it, Samuel says. When you just really get in there.

Jean sits up and Tom stops, allowing two green players to overtake him, then Tom turns swiftly the other way. He paces up the centre and the defenders struggle to get back into position. Jean flicks his hand and they falter. Tom is more than halfway up the pitch and there is not so far to go now. Out of nowhere another green shirt snaps into view. Jean leans to the left before bouncing right; Tom feints left and moves around the opposition. Now it is just an expanse of grass and the goalkeeper before him. Jean capitalises on the goalkeeper's fear, pushing Tom farther forward and faster. Because the goalkeeper is nothing; the goalkeeper is mere flesh.

Amazing, Samuel says, and Jean almost replies, Thank you.

Around him boys and teachers are on their feet. They howl and wail, voices loud and unrestrained, and Jean feels it swell in him too. Tom's pride mixes with his own, twisting from his groin to his lungs. Can Tom feel this too? Someone slaps him on the back, another boy ruffles his hair. Jean does not usually like being touched in this way—roughly and without warning—but finds he does not mind now. Tom is being held aloft by the Compton players, who chant, Manor, Manor Boys (to the tune of "Lou, Lou, Skip to my Lou") and fling him into the air. As Tom lifts up, he turns. Is he looking at Jean? Is he waving, or are his arms simply outstretched for balance? Something flickers in Jean's heart, then Tom is on the ground again. Samuel grabs Jean and whispers softly, voice choked with emotion:

Yes, boys.

They do not win, but they do not lose as badly as they might have. The Brighton team celebrates by pulling their shirts over their heads and ramming into one another. Their teacher screams at them from the sidelines. The Compton players are brought together by David, who is also the coach. David shakes their hands. Jean imagines what he will be saying: Good game, a fighting spirit, great teamwork.

One of the boys leans outside the huddle and shouts at the retreating team and although David pulls him back, the Brighton boys have already turned and are striding onto the pitch. The offending Compton player breaks free from David's grasp and meets his opponent with force. Both teams are there, red over green, green over red, falling in a heap on the ground. The Compton students around Jean surge forward, and he with them, like a rolling wave. The boys are barefooted and bare-armed with uncombed hair: They look, despite the Brighton boys' ill-fitting kit, far wilder and more unkempt, and as they howl down the hill, the opposition meets them with the grim-faced assurance of an army facing barbarians. But as Jean reaches the pitch, he is met by David who warns him: Don't you dare.

Gordon *Gory* Richardson, the maths and biology teacher and David's assistant coach, and the Brighton teachers intercept players, shepherding them away. Jean is caught off guard by David, annoyed that it is only him whom David singles out. Charles Burrows stands on the top steps looking down. He is wearing his purple spectacles and fluorescent orange shorts. He is smiling, watching the boys fight as if this is the game he really came for.

Samuel limps over, grinning. His lip is cut and his shirt muddy. The Brighton team is being herded onto the bus and the Compton players disperse up the hill into various groups. Tom has his arm around someone, his face flushed, happy. As they come toward Jean, one begins singing, softly at first, then louder.

And did those feet, in ancient time . . .

Samuel joins in, and Jean turns his attention to the grass.

Walk upon Englands mountain green?

Jean rips up a dandelion by its root as the sound grows around him. Tom throws himself on the ground and shouts the final line, his voice hot and breathless.

Come on, Yid, Hugo says. Where's your solo?

Tom rolls onto his back. Give us one, he gestures to Jean's cigarette.

You mute? Hugo absentmindedly snatches Samuel's chocolate bar. Oh, I forgot. They don't teach hymns at synagogue.

The joy Jean felt in the game and the adrenalin from the fight turn into damp panic. He cannot look at Hugo. Hymns are a whole other bald patch in his knowledge.

He wasn't mute in the game. Should have seen him, Samuel titters, rocking back and forth in exalted mimicry.

Jean flushes and stares at Samuel, his embarrassment deepening. Fucking Samuel. Jean only sat with him to be nice, and the bastard has turned on him. Jean isn't surprised. Samuel must be as excited as Jean is uneasy to be sitting with The Larks. Jean wants to leave but knows that if he does, it will be worse; if he leaves now, it will be like giving a free pass to everyone and anyone. He has busted too many knuckles and split too many lips to do that. Hugo is the only person who really takes the piss out of Jean and that is because Hugo is built like a brick shit house. Last year they fought, and Jean lost a tooth.

You see that foul? Tom rolls onto his front and flicks ash.

Hugo takes one of Jean's cigarettes and pockets the rest of the packet. Fuckers, he says.

The other boys join in with gusto.

If Davey wasn't there . . .

You'd what?

What wouldn't I do, that's the question.

You couldn't even take on Gory.

Gory used to box.

Heavyweight champion in fifty-five.

Hugo may or may not have said something about their mothers.

Yeah, baby. Whores, every last one of them. Trust me, I've been to Brighton.

The others laugh, high-pitched and nervous, as Hugo stands, demonstrating exactly what he did, or would do, to their mothers. His shorts are bunched around his thighs and his bare chest is muscled and fleshy.

You've got an audience, Tom says, nodding to the younger boys nearby who cackle and whoop. Beyond them, David and Gordon frown through their conversation, arms crossed. Jean does not like Gordon. Gordon has a picture of the queen and another of Churchill in his classroom. He insists on calling the boys by their surnames and when he first learned Jean's, he stumbled: How queer, he said. A Kraut.

Maybe Gory wants to join in.

Maybe you should ask.

Hugo thrusts his hips in a surprisingly lithe way, gyrating and moaning, one hand stretched out pressing down on an imaginary back, as if his imaginary partner is bent over, as if he is fucking her from behind. As if he is fucking her in the arse.

Hugo catches Jean looking and grins.

Or are you going to show us, Yid?

Is there another reason, Jean wonders, that Hugo picks on him? Football, billiards, and pranks are not the only traditions Jean forgoes at Compton Manor; there are also the activities that take place late at night in the back toilets. Jean knows what you can get, or give, if you go there. Everyone does, even Charles. (Jean recalls his definition of *faggot.*) Jean isn't vain, but he is aware that he is not ugly. He has grown up with people—women, men, boys—looking at him. Hasn't Rosa always called him her beautiful boy? He wishes he looked normal. His fists, then, have protected him in more ways than one. Since he is now in the upper sixth, taller, and with more muscle, he is less vulnerable. Perhaps Hugo senses this and perhaps he resents it. Hugo who, rumour has it, spent his younger years on his knees in the back toilets and who now calls boys there himself.

Of course, it is all rumour. None of this would be said aloud. No one is, nor ever will be, a faggot. Hugo is also supposed to have fucked every girl in the village. He goes to town on Saturdays, sometimes to Brighton. He has a subscription to *Playboy* that David doesn't know about.

You know, Hugo says, zoning in on Jean. It's kind of you to grace us with your presence.

Come on, Tom says, quietly, and Hugo's face twitches.

Jean, Hugo says, his lips curled into a smirk. That's a girl's name, isn't it? The others snigger. Am I wrong?

Jean may have a German surname, but his first name is French. It is true that in English *Jean* is the name of a woman. Only Rosa uses the French pronunciation. Everyone else says it the English way, and Jean does not correct them.

You can't even play, Hugo says.

Leave him alone, Tom says, stretching languidly on the grass.

Watch closely, Hugo says to Jean, resuming his gyrating position. You might learn something.

Alright, Tom waves his hand, You look like you're taking a shit.

While Hugo has been talking Jean has kept his face blank, careful not to look directly at him. But now he can't help it, he snorts and Hugo flushes red.

Oh right, one ride and you think you're an expert? Hugo says.

Shut up, Tom says.

Haven't you heard, lads? Tom's been shagging Millie.

Now Tom turns pink, flicks his cigarette onto the grass. He makes modest noises of assent as the others clamour for more details. Adrenalin drains through Jean like sand in an egg timer.

Don't be shy, Peterson.

Millie.

What I would give for an hour with that arse.

What would you take, Tom?

Alright—

Apparently she has a tight, wet—

Alright—

Apparently, she's fucked every man and his—

I'm warning—

Sure you haven't got the clap—

No shame here, my friend.

Tom squares up to Hugo. Eyes locked to eyes, nose to nose. Their sweaty foreheads almost touch, their bare torsos flecked with grass are inches from each other. Years ago, apparently, a French teacher had an affair with a student. It was quiet, impassioned, involving Marxist theory and late-night rallies, and resulted in the teacher and student leading a revolt to overthrow the school board. Since then, relations between boys—and, of course, between boys and teachers—have not just been frowned upon but seen as a direct threat. If boys are found in compromising positions, that is another surefire way to get expelled. For all

David's hippie bullshit and, Jean suspects, his own sexual preferences, he is conservative. The muscles in Hugo's jaw tense, and it seems like he will hit Tom, but then he smirks. His eyes flick from Tom to Jean, and his smile widens.

I get it, he says, crossing an arm over his chest, grinning at Jean. Yeah, I get it.

Jean stays very still, the heat on his face turning cold. He has tried these past two years to keep himself separate, to avoid the very thing Hugo is about to say. To preserve his dignity because—because it is true? Because if he were to go to the toilets, he would never want to leave. The other boys watch attentively, nervous smiles creeping across their faces. Tom's back is to Jean, and although Jean can no longer see his face, he can see the muscles in his neck. Jean is annoyed, suddenly, that Tom came up to him, both three weeks ago and earlier today. Tom has dragged Jean, heart first, into this cesspit. Jean waits for it, as they all do. Waits for Hugo to call him that name and break him apart. But Hugo licks his lips and laughs, prancing back in a surprisingly camp way to deliver his punchline to Tom, not Jean: You, my boy, are a virgin.

The laughter is tinged with hysteria, hiding the others' fear, their relief. Jean laughs too, thankful that is all Hugo has to say. When Jean was home at Easter he tried to have sex with Kelly. She lives, quite literally, on the other side of the tracks in one of the new tower blocks by Shepherd's Bush. Gazing out from her fourteenth-floor window, Jean and Kelly had smoked fags and drank cheap beer. Later, they'd taken off their clothes in her mother's bedroom (her mother who worked double shifts as a cleaner) but even when Jean closed his eyes, he could not do it.

Tom registers that Jean is laughing and something flicks across his face.

Nah mate, Tom says.

You're among friends, Hugo says.

I'm no virgin, Tom says.

Listen, I'll give you some pointers later. Hugo claps an arm around Tom.

Tom squints at the sky. Don't feel bad.

Get Gory's biology books out.

Millie told me fat blokes aren't her type.

It is Hugo's turn to guffaw now.

Trust me, Tom smiles shyly, You're missing out.

Hugo rubs Tom's chest. You hear that, boys? We're missing out!

Jean tries to count the blades of grass. Tom has had sex. With a girl. Why couldn't he have fucked Kelly like she wanted him to, like Tom has fucked Millie? Then he, too, could say he'd done it. Why did Rosa name him after a girl?

Samuel produces a magazine from his bag. From where he is sitting, Jean can see the woman, legs splayed, tits bare, the strange, hairy pocket between her legs, and is reminded, again, why he couldn't do it. The other boys crowd, silent with devotion. Theo breaks it: You can see her arsehole! Hugo snatches the magazine and Samuel chases him, and the others follow, leaving Tom and Jean on the grass.

Jean fumbles for what to say. There is something coiled in his chest, making it hard to breathe.

Guess the match was a bit of a battering, he says, trying to find common ground.

Tom laughs, a harsh bark.

What would you know?

Jean has the feeling he has said the wrong thing, so he says nothing.

And where the fuck were you when it was going down? Tom spins on him. I saw you standing around. Hugo is right, you are a fucking pansy.

Jean blinks back the insult. Something rises in him.

Can you even have sex, he says.

Fuck you.

Don't you piss yourself? Jean knows this will get Tom, who is so sensitive about his epilepsy.

To the side Jean can see Samuel catch up with Hugo, the magazine tearing in two where he grabs it. Gordon strides toward them, shouting. David is watching Jean and Tom. Jean recalls his warning. He knows it is different when he hits someone. Rare that he should consider this though; usually he has done it before he realises. He stands, turning to leave, the blood in his veins pumping, fists clenched, but then Tom says:

Your mum is a German whore, which makes you a German bastard.

Instead of walking away, instead of sitting on the slope like a pansy, instead of listening to Bruce or David or any of the voices that tell him to stop, Jean slams into Tom.

V

THE LETTER ARRIVED THAT MORNING. A LONG GREEN ENVELOPE with purple handwriting. Jean turned it over, wondering who it could be from. Nothing about it was Rosa: not her style. Kelly? Would she fuck. Kelly's handwriting and spelling are worse than his. He heard she has a boyfriend now, older, a musician.

This letter was different—heavy, serious. When he pressed it to his face, the crisp edges of the envelope were sharp and good against his cheeks and when he smelled it—musk and cinnamon—he knew who it was from. Jean was surprised, Micky hadn't written to him for a long time; he used to send the odd postcard from tour, but those stopped in Jean's second term. Jean hasn't spoken to Micky for a year at least, not since that last awful time they saw each other. As Jean pressed the letter to his face, he imaged what Micky might have written: a song, an apology, a love letter? One of the boys in his dorm walked in then and saw him with the unopened letter to his face: That's not how you read, dumbo.

Crack.

Jean swings his pick and brings it down hard on the slab of rock in front of him. As punishment for *attacking* Tom, he has been tasked with breaking rocks at the site of what will be the new swimming pool. Tom has a black eye and a split lip and does not need to break rocks. Why, David did not say. The teeth marks where Tom bit Jean are, three days later, beginning to fade. The physical effort needed to break the rocks makes the blood pump around Jean's body in a way that is not dissimilar to when he fights. Clouds, the same colour as the yellow-grey stone before him, gather. After two weeks of endless heat and a perfect sun, British summer has arrived at last. He swings and brings his pick down, hard, on a particularly large slab of rock, imagining he is a god, the rock a cloud, the sound, thunder.

Even though the sky promises rain, it is still warm, and Jean is drenched in sweat. The swimming pool will be toward the east of the school where currently there is nothing but fields, hedgerows, trees, and the long drive. The drive so deep with gravel that it is not uncommon for cars—mostly the sleek cars of visiting families—to get stuck. The hole for the swimming pool has been dug, but this area is made of Wealden Clay—sandstone, mudstone, siltstone, ironstone, and even, David explained, some limestone. The sandstone, mudstone, and siltstone could be broken down more easily by the digger. The ironstone David saves for the pottery studio. The limestone is more difficult and needs to be split into small chunks before it can be transported. David doesn't know what they will do with it yet. Sell it, use it for the swimming pool construction. David is a big believer in physical labour as a way of strengthening the mind. He told Jean that Ruskin built roads. Jean doesn't need to build a road to know that he should *love thy neighbour.* He knows he shouldn't have hit Tom; he'd do it again.

Wealden Clay dates back to the Hauterivian and Barremian times. In other words, it is one hundred and twenty-five million years old. As Jean breaks the rocks, he contemplates this: how he is literally cracking through time.

The letter had a postage stamp from a week ago, which meant that as Jean read it, he was also experiencing something from the past. Which meant that Micky was already speeding away from him into the future, enacting what in the letter was still only a promise. And another rock splinters.

In 1969, when Mick Caro moved to Queen's Court, Holland Park, he had not yet reached the echelons of fame he now, in 1976, enjoys, but he was well-known enough that the streets in a half-mile radius were ablaze with excited chatter. Jean, having begged Rosa for the latest EP that Christmas, must have listened to it a thousand times leading up to Micky's arrival. Rosa, stirring something on the stove, muttered that it was a sign a place was going downhill when celebrities moved in, and why couldn't they leave the real artists alone?

Because Queen's Court was a cul-de-sac, any traffic directed there had to go down Clemens Gardens where Jean and Rosa lived. It was this that sent Rosa crackers: whole droves of builders who arrived at five in the morning in the backs of trucks and who, it was true, seemed to have no sense that other people were asleep before dawn. The drilling that started promptly at five fifteen, the incessant banging and clanging, the sawing, the brick dust that astonishingly wafted from several streets away into their kitchen, and worse, into Rosa's studio, coating everything in a fine layer of sticky pink. The graveyard of cigarette butts in the gutter.

In the three months before Micky's arrival, Rosa became so irate that Jean thought when he did finally move in, she might go over and whack him around the head with her Le Creuset saucepan. The building works woke Jean up, too, but rather than make him want to *tear my fucking hair out* like Rosa, they filled him with a bubbling sense of wonder. It sounded as if hell itself was being ripped up and remodelled, and it was this, his sense that another world was being created, his inability to imagine what that would look like, that increased his anticipation.

After the building works came the removal van, thundering down their street and turning the corner one damp October morning. A crowd gathered as strange objects were unloaded and brought into the house: a blushing red sofa in the shape of lips, a tall, plastic orange thing that might have been a lamp, several pieces in chrome and leather, and an array of wooden sculptures—figures entwined together, a large phallic gourd—that led neighbours to blush and scoff, and some to tut disapprovingly. The Bechstein. Shrouded in layers of cloth, it was levered through the living room windows by a small crane. Then the car pulled up, a new Aston Martin Lagonda, matt silver, its futuristic glamour totally out of place on a street of Morrises, Fiats, and Mini Coopers, some unknown music—was it Indian?—spilling out its open windows. And, finally, Mick Caro.

To ten-year-old Jean he could have come from another planet. Micky stood in the middle of the street looking up and down, admiring his new home and, also, Jean thought, allowing himself to be admired. Certainly there was much to goggle at. The white shirt open to his stomach. His suede waistcoat, bell-bottom jeans and, shockingly, bare feet right there on the dirty pavement. His smooth, dark hair was long, reaching to his elbows and he was clean-shaven save for the impressive sideburns that curled around his face. Although Jean has never known Micky's exact age, Micky must have been in his late thirties at the time, maybe even early forties. But whereas Rosa, at forty-seven, seemed positively ancient even back then, Micky seemed ageless. He radiated energy. Even the way he stood, flicking cigarette ash with one hip jutting out, was exciting and out of place. Rosa stormed back inside to *do some real work*. The other children clamoured around Micky, wanting to climb into the car, asking for autographs, sweets, anything. But Jean stayed where he was, pressed against a camellia bush, the flowers tickling his cheeks, too curious and too afraid to approach.

Was it this, Jean's reticence, Rosa's refusal to acknowledge Micky, or was it simply Micky's politeness that made him, the next day, show up on their doorstep? He had come, he told Jean, to introduce himself. From her studio, Rosa shouted was it the show-off from round the corner and, if so, could Jean tell him she was busy, and Jean blushed in embarrassment. When he worked up the courage to look at Micky, he saw, to his amazement, that the older man was blushing, too, which made him seem suddenly vulnerable, human. He was having a party, Micky said, for everyone in the area. There would be cake and fizzy pop and it would be lovely if they came.

The chink in the armour Jean witnessed that day was not an anomaly. The thing about Micky was, despite the pomp and the glamour, despite the hippie clothes and long hair, despite the ludicrous house (when Rosa and Jean went round for the party, they wandered disoriented along the hallway that was painted completely bloodred—floor, ceiling, walls, like an artery—and emerged blinking into the chrome and white kitchen), despite his sometimes thoughtless excitement (Micky opening his arms and saying, You came! before discarding Rosa's homemade lemon tart on the side), despite all this, Micky was kind.

During the party he spoke to everyone, including the batty old woman who lived two streets over and smelt faintly of cat piss and garlic; the partially deaf war veteran who shouted about his swollen prostate; the Pakistani couple who had recently set up shop and who wouldn't let their children eat anything; all the mothers; all the children. He told everyone to call him Micky; Rosa opted for Michael, still does. He made a point of saying hello when he passed his neighbours, remembered everyone's names, and made it clear that his home was open to anyone, anytime.

It was only Jean who really took advantage of this hospitality, though, being the only child, it seemed, whose mother worked and who, therefore, had nothing to do for the interminable stretch between school ending and Rosa returning. At first, Rosa was reluctant, a reluctance born as much of embarrassment as suspicion. But Micky charmed her with little gifts—an orchid, a bottle of olive oil from Italy—and his softly spoken voice. He remembered details about her life, asking how teaching was going, what was she working on, and would she like to try a new Bordeaux, he had bought too many bottles. Surely, Jean heard Rosa reasoning with Dinah over the phone, even though Michael was a pompous wretch, and she didn't *really* like him, it was better that Jean was with him than on the streets? Jean thought so: milk and biscuits trumped empty cupboards any day.

Jean doesn't know when he started staying longer. Was it that Rosa taught more evening classes, working later more often, or was it simply that Jean felt more comfortable in Micky's home than in his own? But Jean does know that when Micky got a new Linn LP12 turntable and four Advent speakers (all the way from America, no less), he invited Jean to help install them.

Jean was almost eleven, and Micky had been living round the corner for six months. The gear had been deposited in Micky's sprawling lounge and the large cardboard boxes stood there like strange coffins. Micky could have got his technicians to set it up but, he told Jean, he didn't trust anyone with his acoustics.

The sound, Micky said, hefting a box from the stack, They always fuck up the sound.

Micky split the cardboard with a knife and foam peanuts spilled out like pale, aerated guts. It was Jean's job to collect the peanuts and put them in a black rubbish bag, while Micky packed down the boxes and shifted their contents. While they worked, Micky chatted about the delicacy needed when setting up a high-tech sound system. He often spoke to Jean like this, telling him about something he had just read, a book on Tao philosophy, or a song he was working on, like Bob Dylan but not. Everyday things that were on his mind, an unfiltered monologue. Jean said very little in response. But he had the impression that this was the very reason Micky liked talking to him. Sound, Micky continued, was very personal. Mutable. You needed to know how to put it together. Something, he told Jean, he learned from his dad.

He worked in a bank, Micky said, frowning as he struggled

against the packing tape of another box. But he was obsessed with music.

After Micky had unpacked the boxes, and Jean had stuffed the squishy peanuts into the bag, the texture of the foam in his hands making his teeth hurt, Micky arranged two speakers on shelves at one end of the room, and two at the other.

You want to have these high up, Micky said. So you feel like you're in it.

Micky slid the Linn LP12 record player, the absolute best in the business, he told Jean, onto a black, lacquered sideboard, and arranged the amp on a shelf underneath. The room was dark, like much of the house, painted a deep aubergine colour that made Jean feel sleepy. In the middle of the floorboards was a rug made from a tiger.

He's sick now, Micky said, fixing cables into slots. My father. We haven't spoken in years.

Jean was silent, looking at the stripes of the tiger and Micky's long fingers. They danced over an array of holes, plucking and plugging, working quickly. Jean already felt confused about what went where. He felt panicked, too, because of this subject of fathers, knowing that soon would come the inevitable questions about his own. He never got used to the way someone, a child or teacher at school for example, would ask him what his father did, the cloud that came over their face when he said he didn't have one. Their attempts to console him, was his father dead, had his parents been married long, and then their embarrassment when they finally realised. He'd been waiting for this with Micky; this moment that would change him in Micky's eyes forever.

But Micky didn't probe. Instead, he stood back, inspecting his work, using a cloth to wipe down the record player, the amp, the speakers, and continued to talk about his own father. His father's family came from Lithuania, his mother's from Russia, close to a hundred years ago. Micky was himself, he smiled ruefully, a straight shot of Jew. His ancestors on both sides settled in the East End and for years worked on rag trade factory floors. Then Micky's father got a job as a banking clerk. First one in the family to join the ranks of white-collar workers, to own a house and, eventually, a car. They moved to Golder's Green. Micky's mother, a small, quiet woman, volunteered at the local synagogue. Micky grew up trailing her through the most boring brick houses of London's Garden Suburbs. When he told his parents he wanted to play music, his mother burst a hernia, literally, and his father threw him out.

My father wanted me to be a doctor, Micky said. A lawyer. But it was the old git who bought me my first piano. Who took me to concerts.

Micky laughed, deep and throaty, and when he caught Jean's eye, he smiled.

His father was a proud man and never changed his surname like so many others. When Micky did, his father saw it as another betrayal. But Mick Caro had a better ring to it than Michael Baruch Wilner. Micky wasn't ashamed, he wanted Jean to know that. He never denied his roots—Caro wasn't exactly English—but if journalists suspected he was Italian, Spanish, or Portuguese, he didn't correct them.

Let's see now, Micky said, pulling a record from the shelves that lined the opposite wall. How about Bach?

He popped the record onto the turntable and flicked a few switches, but when the needle touched the black liquorice round, only the snowfall of static came through the speakers.

Micky twisted his lips in frustration, running his hands through his hair, snagging the thick locks and pulling them upward. He bent behind the amp, and as his T-shirt rode up, Jean could see the dark crevice between his buttocks.

It was hell at first, Micky told Jean, as he rearranged wires: he had no money and no place to live. He slept on people's sofas, once on the street, but the point was, and this he wanted Jean to remember, he turned, a wire hanging limply from his hand to gesture, the point was he never gave up. There was something guiding him, laying out this path before him. In many ways he was Buddhist before he was actually Buddhist, you dig.

This was in the fifties when jazz and blues were the things, and he was still Michael. He got a gig accompanying an old girl in the Soho clubs. Those were fun years, spilling in and out of rooms, music tinkling and whining into the early hours—he actually met Count Basie once—but then his singer died, and Micky was alone again. He fell apart for a while in the early sixties but something happened—he lost someone, who, he never said—so he kicked the hard drugs and started to write his own music. Influenced by jazz but, also, by the cool shit that was coming from kids half his age. He didn't have big hopes; just wanted to make enough money to live.

Originally he wrote for other people but no one wanted his music, so he had to sing it himself. Then a song was picked up by a local radio station, and when Dusty Springfield did a cover, he was set. Even when he was doing well, though, his father disapproved. He wouldn't talk to him. Refused, even, to welcome him for Friday night supper.

Micky clicked something and suddenly the deep, sonorous notes of Bach's Cello Suite No. 1 in G Major, played by André

Levy, filled the room (Jean knew it was this because Rosa, too, loved this record). The sound seemed to dance between the walls, flinging itself toward the ceiling. Micky stood, eyes closed, in the middle of the room. The tiger beneath his feet, on the walls, psychedelic paintings of what looked like jungles. Then Jean felt it too. The vibrations in his bones, the rasp of bow against string rippling through his stomach, the sound echoing from the bulb of the instrument and reverberating in his chest. When it was over, Micky opened his eyes, took the needle off, and settled in one of his low cowhide chairs with a cigarette.

The thing I've learned, Micky said, turning the words over, Is that your family is not always . . . your family.

Jean was on the sofa opposite, the leather sticking to his bare legs. He said nothing, the panic in his stomach churning to something else.

What I mean is, sometimes we choose who our family is, Micky said. I don't want to be like my dad.

Micky smoked; Jean sat. Then Micky sprang up and studied the wall of records. What shall we listen to next, my dude?

After that, Jean didn't feel shy about going to Micky's. He went there most evenings, spreading across the tiger's belly, while Micky sat on the low leather sofa. They played record after record—classical, pop, and obscure jazz, sometimes even weirder things that came from far away, and that Jean didn't have language for—Micky commenting on the lyrics here, the refrain there, both of them cocooned in a blanket of sound. Sometimes Micky played himself, the pure hit of piano keys a shock after the overwhelming rush of the hi-fi. Jean felt as if his ribs were being pressed as Micky hummed softly.

The first time Micky drove Jean to school, Jean was excited. There was the car itself, this boxy, gleaming thing with its smooth seats and digital dashboard, like a spaceship, the engine that barely purred as they raced through London. But really it was simply being next to Micky that made Jean's heart swell. The car could have been anything; if Jean was next to Micky, he was protected by invisible armour. He stuck his head out the car window and watched London rush past. Streets that had seemed so large and dirty before were now, from his position of height and speed, beautiful.

When Jean got to school, however, the armour disappeared. Rather than help Jean, Micky's presence made things worse. Before, Jean was tolerated at best, at worst, ignored. Too slight for sport, too stupid for class, too angry for friends, now he became something different. Dangerous. Boys shoving him into the games cupboard and locking the door. Pressing his face into gravel. Smacking the back of his head with a ruler. Jean could have asked Micky to drop him around the corner so others wouldn't see, or taken the bus like everyone else, but that would have been a betrayal of everything he and Micky had together.

By this point, Jean was so deeply in love with Micky that he would have done anything for him. He didn't need other friends; he had Micky. Micky, who taught him so much more than any boy his own age ever could. Micky who, when Jean was eleven, showed him the wonders of meditation and Bruce Lee. Who later, when Jean was twelve, introduced him to the magic of hashish, ripping a hole in the fabric of Jean's reality and stitching him a new one. Jean would have rather died than tell Micky about the boys who hurt him; instead he sat, faithfully, loyally, in the front of the car, knowing Micky would be there in the evening, and in the morning, Micky would drive him to school.

Jean was important to Micky too. Is that not why Micky wrote him a song? The song that really shot Mick Caro into the stratosphere so that later, when they arrived at school, Jean now a teenager and far too old to be driven, there was already a gaggle of schoolgirls and mothers waiting for them.

Micky had written the song late at night, just before Jean's thirteenth birthday. It was 1972, three years after Neil Armstrong first walked on the moon, and the world was space mad. Bowie's "Starman," The Kinks's "Supersonic Rocket Ship," King Harvest's "Dancing in the Moonlight," tunes with arrangements to match their cosmic content: synths, violins, backing vocals. Then Micky's small celestial offering: "Boy in Space." Sung with only his piano for accompaniment, part ballad, part nursery rhyme, about two boys who build a spaceship in the garden out of junk. In the night, when one of them cannot sleep, he goes outside to the ship and, miraculously, it fires up, flinging the boy into space.

When Jean first heard the song, sitting in Micky's living room, the last of the summer light fading behind the poplar trees in the garden, he had felt himself become unstuck. It was as if he soared through the ceiling and into the air, and he was reminded of that bit in *Enter the Dragon* when they talk about heavenly glory. The song, to him, was about becoming, about being something else, something greater than himself; it was about the ship they made together, the stars that bound them. Something about the way Micky sang pierced Jean's throat. Long after Micky had finished singing, Jean could not speak. Micky was silent and it seemed to Jean as if they existed in their own dark patch on the surface of the moon.

It is something Jean has held on to all this time. If he has to go back to London, at least there will be Micky. Which is why it hurt, more than Tom's teeth, to read Micky's letter this morning in which he told Jean in strangely formal language that he was moving to Hollywood. The first fat drops fall to the earth, turning the yellow clay brown. Jean picks up his pace.

After David gave Jean his punishment, he softened and said, If you find a bit of dinosaur, you can keep it. Thanks, no thanks. Jean swings down hard. Why is it only him who needs to *strengthen his mind*? Why not Tom or Hugo? Why aren't they building a fucking road or breaking rocks? Jean misjudges and hits the rock at an odd angle. It is resistant, retaliating with a force that judders through Jean's arms. Work is the force acting upon an object to displace it, Jean recalls the definition from physics.

It seemed natural to Jean when his relationship with Micky slipped into something more intimate, as if Jean had been walking in a storm for some time and now, finally, he had found its quiet centre.

It was a few weeks after Micky had written Jean's song. He was throwing Jean a small party for his birthday. There were Rosa and Dinah, Micky and one of his session players. There was a chocolate cake and fruit punch. Jean didn't like eating in front of people, so he only licked a bit of icing. There was a piñata that Jean thwacked ineffectually, the frictionless air making him lose balance. It was Dinah, in fact, who clobbered the thing, hollering with surprising force and smashing it even after it lay destroyed on the ground. Everyone had a good time; Rosa, remarkably, was not rude, and left with a large chunk of cake.

Jean stayed, ostensibly to help Micky clean up, but when the door shut, he lounged on the sofa, knowing now they would smoke.

Instead of rolling the usual joint, though, Micky passed him a cut-crystal glass with a puddle of golden liquid in it. Happy Birthday, he said.

Jean's eyes watered and he coughed most of the whisky onto himself. Micky was wearing strange, low-slung cotton trousers that looked like something between pyjamas and a skirt. They were hareem pants, he had explained to the party earlier, from his trip to India. They had slipped lower, revealing the dark band of flesh between his shirt and underwear. Jean gazed at his glass, took another sip, forced himself to swallow. It still tasted awful, but a warmth radiated down his throat and through his chest.

Micky watched Jean from where he stood by the kitchen island, a smile playing across his mouth.

You have a good time? he said, and Jean curled his lips, shrugged. Hard man to please, Micky said.

Jean drained his glass and breathed fire. I get tired, he said.

Me too, Micky said. People suck. Other people.

The whisky made Jean feel both lighter and denser. He sank into the sofa, he wanted to dance. It was a warm early summer evening.

I've got an idea, Micky said. Let's meditate.

He took off his shirt and trousers and sat on the floor. Jean blinked at the thrill of it—he had seen Micky like this before, of course. Always when they meditated (Micky said it was important to be as comfortable as possible). But if, in these moments, Jean felt a twinge in his abdomen, he ignored it. The whisky made him bold and now he took Micky in.

Micky was different up close compared with photographs in

magazines. He was shorter, and his body not as firm. What Jean loved most were the thick, dark, locks that were so different from his own flat hair. The long sideburns that stopped abruptly.

Come on, Micky said. Jean obliged, undressing like Micky had, and plonking himself on the vinyl, smiling stupidly.

Be serious, Micky said.

But after what seemed like only seconds Jean opened his eyes. This time he was close enough to see the texture of Micky's skin, the moles scattered across his chest. There was something fragile about him that made Jean want to bury his face in the three soft folds of his stomach. Here, the hair was paler, almost blond, tapering to nothing at the waistband of his shorts. The thrill revolved darkly in Jean's stomach. He wanted more whisky; his mouth was dry. His eyes trailed lower and there was the gaping hole of Micky's shorts, through which he could see more hair and the dark puckered skin of something. Instinctively Jean wanted to touch it. The heat prickled his forehead, sweat slid into his eyes, and when he blinked up, Micky was watching him.

Jean, Micky said. Jean could not read the expression in his eyes. Was he also afraid? Micky's cheek twitched; he didn't move. He didn't close his legs. Jean, he said again, but this time gone was the warning.

And Jean knew then that Micky wanted to touch him too.

They didn't though. No, there was never anything like that between Micky and Jean. Instead, Micky closed his eyes, and Jean did too. After, Micky suggested they take a shower to cool off. This is what happened: Micky and Jean, side by side, bent over the marble tub, Micky massaging soap into Jean's hair, his strong fingers pressing pleasingly on Jean's scalp.

The intimacy Jean felt came from something unspoken and

unrealised; a desire that coiled below his groin. Something that bound them together. That is what Micky said, isn't it, in his song: They were best friends, comrades, space travellers hurtling through the galaxy.

All this is to say, yes, they smoked and drank and meditated and bathed, but nothing ever *happened*. Nothing Jean could put his finger on and say, this.

Which means Jean is still a virgin.

It is true that over these past two years, since being at Compton Manor, Jean has grown more distant from Micky—they haven't spoken for a year—but it is also true that, now that Micky is gone, Jean realises how much he meant to him. Micky was a comfort Jean assumed would always be there. The song, each time it plays, is a promise.

Jean tightens his grip on the pick and brings it down, hard, and this time, the rock splits. The rain slides down his face. He places the pick to one side and squats. There, where the rock is split, lies the exposed and wriggling body of a worm. It is fat and pink and jerks from side to side.

And now Micky is gone. And now—Jean slices the worm in half—Tom is no longer his friend.

When the rain gets excessive, creating rivulets of dark brown by his feet, sticking his hair to his face, and running cold down his back, Jean goes to the farm.

Since his fight with Tom, he is back with the pigs. He says hello and apologises for having been gone so long. Salome, Elizabeth II, and Muhammed Ali huddle under their shelter, indifferent. Their names were chosen by popular vote when the pigs were brought to the farm, although Jean isn't sure who voted for Salome apart from David. He remembers when Mo was found riding Sally, and David squealed, There's sex in the pig pens! The boys sniggered, That's not the first time, looking at Hugo. The pigs are used for their eating capabilities. Garden scraps, food waste, and, when the lawnmower is broken, grass. Until of course the day that they're not. They are Tamworth pigs, light brown in colour with pert, intelligent ears. Well, usually they are light brown; currently they are covered in dark, thick shit.

Alright lads, Jean says. What's been going on?

Lizzie and Sally grunt. Mo wanders off.

Sorry, Jean says. *Ladies.*

Jean considers washing the pigs first, but that will make the rest of the pen wet, and he doesn't want to shovel liquid shit. He fills their feeders and watches their dirty behinds shuffling for space. Pigs have a reputation. Some people assume they are dirty because they are stupid when in fact it's the opposite. Pigs, like any other animal, attract flies. Unlike other animals, their tails don't bat these away. They roll themselves in whatever cool substance is available. Mud or shit. Jean feels guilty for leaving the pigs for the chickens.

The rain bounces off the tin roof, creating a cacophony of sound. It hammers out thoughts of Micky and lets Jean focus on shovelling shit into the wheelbarrow. Clearing space in his mind as he clears space on the floor. There is room, again, for his thoughts to wander. *It's raining cats and dogs*, they would say. When Jean was younger, he wanted to know where that phrase came from. He would watch the rain and imagine that each droplet contained a tiny furry creature. The dogs howling, the cats mewling. He deposits the barrow's contents in the compost, which will be used in the kitchen gardens, the ornamental gardens, and the flower beds. Outside, the rain isn't as heavy as it sounds.

Jean learned, years later in Charles Burrows' class, that the phrase came from the medieval era when cats and dogs slept under the eaves. Rain would seep through the thatched roofs and onto the sleeping animals, forcing them from their places of rest. Down they climbed, an avalanche of cats and dogs, into the realm of the human.

Jean fills up another load of manure. When he first came to the farm, the stink made him gag, but he is used to it now.

It's raining cats and dogs isn't about what the rain is but about what the rain does, then.

It is funny how meaning slips around. It is how people talk: saying one thing but meaning another. Jean finds it hard to understand people most of the time.

Like when Micky says he'll always be there but moves to America. Like when David says he cares but makes Jean break rocks. Like when Rosa says she loves him but is crying. Like when Tom calls him a bastard.

Although Jean has tried to keep the fact of Rosa a secret, he knows the other boys know. When he and Tom were by the lake and Tom was complaining, again, about his father, Jean said, I hate my father too.

Tom looked at him funny then and said, quite clearly, I don't hate my father.

Jean blushed and explained that neither did he, how could he when he didn't even know his father.

And Tom looked at him in an even stranger way, curling his top lip and pulling his eyebrows back. To cover his embarrassment, Jean told Tom about Micky. The Aston Martin and home cinema and special Mexican marijuana. Tom's eyes lit up—he, too, was a fan of Mick Caro, who wasn't?—and Jean promised Tom they'd go for a spin when he visited. A promise Jean can't keep.

Jean retrieves the hose and washes down the pen. Streaks of dark brown fade to reveal the hard, grey concrete beneath.

Now Tom will think Jean is not just a bastard, but a lying bastard.

Jean turns the hose toward the pigs, who shuffle together, trying to avoid the cold jet. The shit softens under the water pressure and runs off their skin like blood. The pigs grunt and whimper. Tom will hate Jean even more, and Jean hates Micky for it. The water runs down the pigs' hides. Jean hates himself for it too. Underneath the feeling of abandonment is the sickly knowledge that it is all his fault.

It was almost a year ago, Jean had just returned from his holiday in Provence with Rosa and was about to go back to Compton Manor. He was sixteen, sitting in Micky's kitchen. They were drinking and smoking. Jean was unusually quiet that night, Micky said, and Jean had sneered. He didn't know at the time why he felt so angry, but when Micky came to him, when Micky stroked his face and said, Little man, what's wrong? Jean snapped his chin away. Later, when Micky wrapped an arm around Jean's shoulder and suggested they take a shower, Jean flung him away, smacking Micky's face with the back of his hand. Micky stood frozen, the fear and hurt in his eyes dimming to something darker when Jean said, Don't touch me, faggot.

Jean trains his jet of water on the pigs now, pressing them against the wall. Their squeals rise in panic, but they can't escape the force of the water. Work is the force acting upon an object to displace it.

Jean didn't see Micky again before he left for school, and when he was back during the holidays, Micky was in Europe or America. Jean had never called anyone a faggot before and was surprised that he had slapped Micky; at the time, Jean had buried the encounter in the back of his mind, assuming things would right themselves. It wasn't even that big a deal.

Jean holds his position, forcing the pigs back on top of one another. He directs the water across them, getting shit off their legs, their hooves, their bellies. They are squealing and Jean can tell they are afraid. He is afraid too: in his letter, Micky did not tell Jean when he would be back. He did not, as he so often promised he would, invite Jean to join him in America. Jean did not know why he was so angry at Micky; he is embarrassed, now, about hitting Micky.

The pigs' hides gleam, but Jean continues to spray them, not stopping when they become frantic, instead training his jet across their faces, not giving them time to recover. He flicks his hand and jets Sally in the eye. She screams, and it sounds human.

When he returns to school, it is lunchtime. He passes Theo, Percy, and Tom. When Jean first arrived at the school, it was Theo he thought would be his friend. Jean was a city boy, unused to this country shit, and when he came upon Theo, the only mixed-race boy in the school, lying on the grass, smoking in the sun, he assumed the same of him.

This is probably why Jean asked confidently if Theo wanted to smoke something stronger and why, when the other boy stiffened, Jean didn't notice; if he had, he wouldn't have gone on to talk about the new Gregory Isaacs and Westbourne Grove and how he couldn't wait to get out of this dump. Theo, voice cold and tight, said he was alright, Thanks mate, and moved away.

After, Theo didn't speak to him again, never directly at least, and Jean didn't try to make new friends. Of course, there was Samuel, but Jean has never counted Samuel as a real friend—it is true that Samuel made similarly wrong assumptions about Jean—and there is Tom. Thinking about it, was it Theo who told Tom about Jean's weed? Theo stays close to Hugo; he laughs hardest at his jokes.

Percy is slight with dark hair and olive skin. He says very little and can't look anyone in the eye. He is, like other boys in the school, prone to outbursts of violence but mainly toward himself. There are scars on his arms. He is the kind of boy that boys like Hugo and Theo would usually bully. But Theo knew Percy from before, so Percy is protected.

Theo holds his nose and Percy looks at the ground.

Fucking hell, Theo says. You're not *actually* meant to fuck the pigs.

Percy laughs, a low stutter.

Tom's eye has blossomed to a dark purple. His lip is swollen. Like a closed bud. He stares at Jean but says nothing.

Charles Burrows' door is ajar, and Jean can hear, unmistakably, the voices of the teacher and Hugo. Charles's voice is raised, Hugo's insistent, but Jean cannot make out the words. Then Hugo bursts out of the room. When he catches sight of Jean, his expression changes, and he barges past, telling Jean to stop fucking staring. But before this, Jean saw something. What was it—happiness? Excitement? As Jean passes Charles's office, he looks through the open door and sees the teacher standing at the window, staring across the grounds.

VI

THE BOYS ARE ALLOWED A PARTY ONCE A TERM AND EVEN though exams are soon, there is one tonight. It is summer solstice, David's favourite time of the year.

Pre-party rituals began last night with David leading the boys to the boating pond, where they jumped in, one after the other. St. John's Day, as it is known in the Christian calendar and, as David refers to it, also marks the birth of John the Baptist. The boys in the water represented the baptism of dead pagan children. Jean knew this because he was listening when David explained; but most of the boys were just hot and excited by the excuse to get wet.

When it came to Jean's turn, he hesitated. It isn't that Jean is religious—he has never celebrated Jewish holidays and, importantly, he is not circumcised—but, somehow, it seemed wrong to join a fake baptism. David was standing at the water's edge, reciting Scripture in a low monotonous tone. It was a warm June evening, the light lingered on the Downs, and midges made the air vibrate. The other boys began to get impatient, and soft clucking behind Jean grew into full-blown chicken squawks. He was aware that all eyes were on him and that he was only in his swimming shorts.

He took a few steps back, leaning into the squabbling boys, then he shifted his weight onto the balls of his feet—the noise around him growing from squawks into yells—and took three long strides down the pontoon, pitching himself forward. His arms came up, his legs clamped together, and he sailed through the air, curving down and cutting into the water with a tinkle. He emerged to the sound of whoops and cheers. Jean hated swimming pools, but holidays by French lakes showed him the joy of swimming. He was good at diving, and he could feel the pleasure and surprise of the other boys.

He caught Tom's eye. The bruise around it, like an ink stain.

It had been ten days since Jean's fight with Tom and a week since his rock-breaking punishment. Jean had spent this time building a force field around himself. The few occasions he had passed Tom in the canteen or in class, and their eyes happened to meet, it was as if Tom looked straight through him and so, too, had Jean's face remained blank.

Then Tom smiled at Jean in the water.

Now that the boys have been *cleansed*, today is devoted to preparations for the party this evening. There is going to be a feast, a fire, and music. And there are going to be girls. It is one of the few times females are admitted onsite, and the air is tense. Boys prowl the grounds. Classes are cancelled and students divided. Jean is on the wood team, gathering branches and chopping logs for the bonfire. The day has been grey so far, but as he layers logs in a hexagonal pattern, the sun emerges, illuminating the structure and making it seem as if already on fire.

Jean remembers watching older boys at previous solstice parties jump over the fire. The anticipation before, the disbelief during, and the exhilaration after. Later, much later, when the fire settled into embers and the sky was properly dark, the younger boys leaped over the smouldering pile to show that they could do it too. Of course, they could; but there is something different about doing it with the whole school watching. This year, since Jean is one of the oldest, he will be part of the ceremony.

There are many ways to celebrate the solstice, David tells them. In Egypt, they have worshipped the sun god, Ra, for thousands of years, and Charles blares Sun Ra all day, as he finishes making the headdresses. When Jean walks past, he sees the teacher, eyes closed, swaying to the music, surrounded by yarn, feathers, leaves, and a pair of ram's horns. His rabbits blink from under the table, eyes like coals.

Last night, after their swim, Cook handed out cocoa in the common room and David said, Did you know that in Italy, the solstice is a very important day for young, unmarried women? David drank from his cup, coating his top lip light brown. They leave a glass of water with an egg white outside, and, in the morning, the shape of the albumen predicts their fortune. A full sail foretells a rich sailor; a sickle, a farm; and a coffin, death.

Did you also know, Charles said after David had gone to

bed, Did you also know that in Italy they drink this fantastic concoction? He passed around the flask—to Hugo first, then the others, Tom, Jean, Percy, Samuel, Colin, and Theo. Jean wasn't a stranger to booze, but even so, he coughed at the bitter, medicinal taste.

You have to pick the walnuts in November when they're unripe, Charles said, And brew the *nocino* for eight months.

The others, Jean was relieved to see, coughed too.

Walnut trees are very powerful, Charles said. They say witches make sacrifices there. You're about to become men. You'll be leaving after the summer. Cheers to that.

They passed around the flask, feeling the liquid burn their throats. Tom's face was pink. He was in his swimming shorts and an old shirt unbuttoned to the stomach, which was striped white and pink like peppermint rock.

David tells them that in antiquity people believed time stood still, the sun stopped moving, and the earth flipped over during solstice. Jean likes this idea, but it doesn't make sense: time stops frequently, not on one day of the year. Whole hours can race past, and Jean will still be in the same spot. David also tells them that the boundary between our world and the magical becomes porous, allowing fairies and sprites to dance freely across. Allowing, too, evil spirits, which must be chased away through song and dance. Again, this is stupid: the line between this world and another has always been thin. How else could Jean communicate with Bruce Lee; how else could he read the signs around him? But Jean is willing to accept that tonight they will have greater access to the magic and that the magic will be of a more potent flavour. Charles tells them about Midsummer Night, which is different but close, and Shakespeare. Men turning into beasts, the moon, brick; they go mad and fall in love with one another; the fairies are not kind, but spiteful.

David tells them that in Chinese thought, the day is considered to be strong with yang energy—the sun, heat, masculinity, chaos, penetration, the south side of a hill, the north bank of a river—and so, particular focus is given to generating more yin energy—the moon, cold, femininity, order, earth, absorption, the north side of a hill, the south bank of a river. David wears a dress, a red fifties number, and lipstick. Some boys raid David's dressing-up box, and Tom, Hugo, Theo, and Percy parade in skirts and blouses, their confident yang energy shining through regardless. Jean decides against it, although he meditated this morning, which helped restore his balance.

A boy, bare-chested with feathers in his hair and a flight of vermillion billowing behind, screaming as he runs down the hill, chased by three others, their faces yellow, green, purple.

Others emerging from the hole for the swimming pool, naked and covered in mud.

Charles sitting on the balconied window ledge, smoking, his mirrored shades glinting in the light.

David leading a line in dance through the fields, banging drums and chanting.

A boy in a wheelchair adorned with flowers and grasses, bombing down the hill, his yelps tinged with terror.

Gordon standing at the forest edge with three others, their bare feet dug into the earth, their arms erect, pretending to be trees.

David, his makeup running with sweat, standing by the hot pit over which Mo's body turns, dark red flesh dripping fat.

The fire Jean has finished building is behind the school, up the hill. Down below, Jean can hear boys practising—the clash of drums and twang of a guitar—and smell the smoky meat. He can see far across the Downs to Furlwood Ridge. Jean loves this view: the way the land dips and rises, the green hills like a child's drawing, scratched with bushes, fingerprints of yellow, and dark patches of forest. In the distance the sea hovers, like a mirage, a pale strip that blends into the sky, bridging earth and heaven. Jean stretches himself, his limbs stiff and aching from squatting. The two younger boys who were helping him have drifted off. Jean wishes it could be like this forever, a day without a setting sun. But he knows that, even if tonight it comes late, the darkness will come.

First, they eat.

The hall has been decked out with switches of willow, the branches hanging transgressively over the austere paintings. The tables have been put together to form a banquet scene. Someone has unearthed tablecloths, the once white lace now yellowed with age. Pools of orange light from thick beeswax candles and strips of wax decorate the surface. There are silver platters of bread rolls and instead of the usual mishmash cutlery, the silver has been brought out, and the real china. The windows seem particularly bright, as if someone has cleaned them, each diamond a deep blue.

When the roast boar is brought in, there is a collective intake of breath. It is displayed whole on a silver platter, surrounded by fruits and vegetables that look like the sun—lemons, oranges, peaches, apricots, squash, corn, tomatoes—and takes eight boys to carry it. They display it, walking stiffly up and then down the length of the table, their cheeks red with exertion and responsibility. Not so many years ago, the pig would have been slaughtered in the main field, its neck slit, its blood collected, its intestines washed and used for sausage casings. Now, due to *boring technical legalities* (David's words), the animal is killed off-site. Tonight, there is a seating plan, and Jean is at the top of the table with the other oldest students. Tonight, David explains, Is not just about the sun, but the passing of boys into men.

Shortly, the boys you see at this table will leave us and head into the world. Let us guide them.

Shouts from the hall. Charles pours nocino into his and Hugo's glasses.

Our family will change, David says, But we are all Compton brothers until the end!

He raises his glass and the school stands, cheering.

Whoever loves his brother lives in the light, and there is nothing in him to make him stumble. But whoever hates his brother is in the darkness, and he walks about in darkness. He does not know where he is going because the darkness has blinded him. Tonight, boys, let us bring them from the darkness and into the light!

The pig is good: moist and tender, and fragrant with garlic and smoke. The boys eat with their hands and fat dribbles down their chins. Tom is on the opposite side of the table, three places to the left of Jean. His mouth is shiny and flecked with bits of meat. When David gets up to do his rounds, Charles leans over and pours nocino into each of the boys' glasses. *Salut!* he says. *Santé!* says Colin. *Nostrovia!* says Tom and Jean's heart jumps. Was the Russian for him? *L'chaim!* Samuel shouts and Jean blushes, avoiding the others' grinning faces as he lifts his glass.

Next, the drum stalk.

Charles returns with the seven headdresses. Samuel is given one made of willow, adorned with roses and ivy. Colin and Theo have wreaths of cherry, decorated with husks of corn and shaves of wheat. Percy's is simple, a band of ribbon with three black feathers; Tom's is the same, but with white feathers; and Jean's has feathers and flowers and fruit. Hugo is given the ram's horns. They are also each given a rune: a leather thong with a small, flat stone, upon which has been carved a strange symbol. Charles explains the meanings in a voice heavy with drink. Most boys have the *Sowilo* symbol, meaning *sun*. A time for joy and abundance, success and prosperity. Hugo kisses his rune and stands to cheers from the hall. Tom has been given *Raidho*, which signifies a *wheel* or *journey*. Jean has been given *Perthro*, which, Charles says, pausing for dramatic effect, means *destiny*.

David leads the boys in single file, the seven oldest at the front, through the hall, singing a low chant—*earth my body, water my blood, air my breath, and fire my spirit*—that grows along the line. Samuel's palm is sweaty in Jean's right, Colin's dry in his left. The procession moves along the corridor, into the entrance hall, through the large, wooden double doors, down the stone steps and the parterres, through the lawns, past the boating pond, and into the open meadow. Here, the seven are blindfolded and left, quite suddenly it seems, alone. The song retreating with muffled footsteps.

Then the drumbeat: loud, sonorous, and distant. Jean takes a tentative step toward it, cocking his head to hear better and disrupting his headdress. The flowers and leaves cover his ears and disorient him.

There's fucking thistles!

As Jean fumbles his way toward the drumbeat, which has increased in speed, he comes closer to and moves farther away from his fellow brothers. He is on his hands and knees; it is easier to navigate with more of his body on the ground. Here the elevation of a mole hill, there the dip, and now, a thick clump of grass. Jean senses the presence of someone nearby and moves away, while still, he hopes, in the direction of the drum. In doing so, he bumps directly into a different boy, their headdresses tangling together. Their hands come up at the same time to feel feathers pressed against feathers, knuckles grazing, fingers interlocking as they silently extricate themselves. It is the smell that identifies the boy to Jean—sweetness of mud, saltiness of meat, and something else, aromatic like rosemary. This is what is meant by magic. Then they are free from each other, the air cool between them. Tom's hand grazes Jean's cheek, brushes his shoulder, finds his hand and squeezes, before he moves away.

After, when they take off the blindfolds, they will laugh about how short the distance is from where they began to the fire. But during, the drum stalk is infinitely long. The drumbeats decrease in volume and frequency, signalling the end of the challenge, and Jean is afraid he will not make it in time. But he does, as do all the others, even Samuel (with some help from two guides), and they emerge, blinking and breathless, to the warmth of the crackling fire and the expectant faces of the school.

Then, the jump.

Jean takes it at a run, leaping with two feet over the flames, emitting a wild, ecstatic cry.

And finally, the party.

The girls are waiting for them in the hall. They are dressed in thin, white cotton slips with flowers in their hair and stand at the edge, watching the boys swagger in. It has been some time since Jean has seen a female (Cook and Matron don't count) and the girls, anxiously playing with their hair, tugging the hems of their dresses, pinching the fat of their midriffs, and leaning, hips jutting out to one side, make him homesick for Kelly.

A girl breaks away and runs toward the boys, hair flowing behind, chest rising with the effort.

Kelly with her stiff Mohican and painted face, wearing nothing but her underwear, a slashed T-shirt, and a pair of steel-toe-capped boots. Kelly with a bottle of some awful mixture that burns his throat and a couple pills that make him woozy. Kelly leading him through the maze of London transport to the most random places—Acton, Bow, London Fields—a shell of a house, its wallpaper peeling, full of smoke and people. Or along a back alley, down some stairs, and into a sweaty box. Kelly dancing ass to groin with men whose blunts are so big it makes Jean high just looking. Kelly who never wakes up before twelve. Kelly who lives off baked beans alone.

The girl Jean recognises as Millie flings her arms around Tom, kissing him on the cheek.

Oi oi!

Kelly would laugh at the girls in their hippie dresses and plaits, especially Millie, whose dirty blonde hair covers her face as she whispers something to Tom. Whose dress rises to reveal fat, pink thighs.

Except Kelly wouldn't. The last time Jean saw her, her naked back was turned away from him as they lay in her mother's bed, the sheets crumpled underneath. The night before, they had seen a ska band play round the corner in Shepherd's Bush. They smoked some hash and drank a litre of rum, and Jean was exceedingly happy to be in that basement club with Kelly. To grip her swaying hips as she pressed against him. Usually he felt self-conscious, aware how tall, lanky, and white he was. Kelly didn't have that problem. Her mum is Irish, but she claims her dad is from Trinidad. Not that she's ever met him. Still, she has always known how to be in those clubs. That night the room was so packed Jean was forced to press against her. The lack of space left no room for his embarrassment. As Kelly pressed against him and as the heat in the room reached fever pitch, men and women half naked from it, Kelly stopped being Kelly. She became someone else; Jean gripped her hips tighter, and she pulled him toward her.

But whatever happened on the dance floor didn't translate to the bedroom. In the expanse of her mother's bed, Kelly became Kelly again. With all the bits of her that he loved; and those that he couldn't. In the morning, she asked him what was wrong with her, and when he didn't answer, told him she didn't want to be his friend anymore.

Millie's head rests on Tom's shoulder, his arm is loosely around her waist. The adrenalin of the day ebbs away from Jean. There is a noise, a squeal that is both human and not, and Salome the pig, followed by David the headmaster, thunder into the hall.

Be not amazed! Be not seduced!

Jean lurks at the back, watching the scene unfold: watching as Millie buries her face in Tom's chest, as Tom's hand soothes her.

David circles the pig around the room once, twice, three times, and drives her down the front steps. After, the cake is brought in, and Jean gets it. Sweet, red jam pools under an iced chin, and berries, purple and pink, in a crushed mess at the edge. It is meant to be John the Baptist. One of David's strange, Christian jokes that no one really understands. There is also jelly, iridescent orbs in pale yellow, green, and orange. Jean is reminded of insects mummified in amber and how, tonight, time is meant to stop. He wishes it would stop as Tom's hand tightens around Millie's waist, as Charles Burrows lurches across the room with punch glasses, as David stands onstage and welcomes the fairy sprites to the most magical night of the year!

The Larks perform: Tom, Theo, and Percy have removed their headdresses but Hugo, the front man, keeps his ram horns. He has drawn a line across his face à la Bowie and bends his body, remarkably lithe, toward the mic. Tom plays the bass, Theo the guitar, and Percy the drums. The youngers, small and spotty, keep to one side, while the older boys venture into the middle. The girls offer the boys the glare of their cheeks, noticing without acknowledging, and both groups move around one another. Led Zepplin, Bowie, Cream, The Kinks, Pink Floyd, and a horrible, horrible rendition of Queen's "Bohemian Rhapsody." Music which Jean wouldn't be caught dead listening to in

London. Which wouldn't happen because it wouldn't be around. Instead, The Clash, Sex Pistols, Ramones, Ed Banger and the Nosebleeds. Bands to whom Kelly introduced him and which they follow with fervour. Kelly has started her own band; she told him about it that night in Shepherd's Bush. Like The Slits but more punk. Who is Kelly's new boyfriend? Jean wonders.

The music is not good, but he likes the way Tom, who is shirtless in his long, patterned skirt, holds the bass below his groin. Tom jumped over the fire, skirt billowing around him, staring at a fixed point ahead, as if looking for someone in a crowd. Tom has the same look now as he plays the bass, and he isn't, Jean realises with satisfaction, looking at Millie. But Millie is staring at Tom.

Then The Larks play Micky's song, "Boy in Space," the one about Jean, and Jean leaves the room.

Her name is Sandra, she goes to the local grammar school, and her cousin, Millie, dragged her along, she tells Jean as they smoke a joint around the back. She was told she had to wear white, and this was the only thing she had, she gestures at her latex dress.

Sandra was actually there in Manchester when the Sex Pistols played. She even had a ticket to the gig, but she got drunk and missed the whole thing. Sandra speaks quietly and quickly so Jean must lean in to hear. Her eyes dart from his face to the ground as she takes short, rapid puffs. She is smaller than Kelly and thinner. Her hair is growing out at the roots and her makeup doesn't suit her face. With Kelly, even though she has had many different looks, each one has always seemed effortless. He can't imagine her younger, without makeup, without the fag or that crushing grin. Sandra adjusts her dress and the fabric squeaks against her skin.

Back inside, The Larks have finished, and they sit on the stage, enjoying the attention. David is with Charles in a corner, his red dress grimy, lipstick faded. Charles's eyes roam lazily. The room is hot and people loom out from its sweaty depths. The cake is overly sweet, so is the punch. Millie is in Tom's arms, swaying to the slow jam. Hugo has his arms around a girl with black hair. Samuel clings to the ample bottom of a girl two feet taller than him, and Jean finds himself dragged onto the dance floor by Sandra.

Jean watches with horrified fascination as Tom and Millie press closer together. His hands slide along her back and hold her arse, and as they turn, Jean can see the bulge in Tom's skirt. He imagines how Millie feels, pressed against Tom, the thickness by her thigh, the solidity of his chest. Sandra's latex is hot against Jean's skin, causing him to sweat. Jean imagines it is not Sandra's body on his, but Tom's, not Sandra's hot hand that curls around his neck, but Tom's. Jean isn't sure who does it first: if he does it so he doesn't have to watch Tom do it, or if he does it because Tom does it, or if he does it so he can be closer to Tom, doing it at the same time, but Tom's tongue is in Millie's throat, her tongue in his; Jean's in Sandra's. He is pretending to be Millie, kissing Sandra and pretending she is Tom.

The moon casts a bright, clear light that makes the fields blue-black and glowing. Jean's shadow drags behind him. It is only when he is halfway across that he realises: The day is over.

Kelly, he reasons, Kelly is his sister. Wasn't it Kelly that day in school who told the others to shove off, kicking one boy in the groin with her formidable boots. After, helping Jean clean his face and taking him to the pub. During those awful years between thirteen and fifteen, Kelly looked after him, skipping school and showing him what she called *real London*.

He tried to explain to Kelly that morning when she turned away from him, her naked body stiff; they *were* siblings. It wasn't right. He could tell she was crying from the way she said, voice choked and tight, Fuck off, Jean.

But Sandra is not his sister. He should have stayed, he should have led her outside, like he watched Hugo do, like he watched Tom do. Instead, he made an excuse about needing the toilet and ran as fast as he could.

The journey to the clearing feels much longer in the dark. At one point Jean considers going back, but when he turns around, he is immediately disoriented. The lake gleams like expensive lacquer next to him. If he follows it to the end, he should—and he does—come upon the clearing. It is like a scene in a play or from a film. Perfectly lit.

After they jumped over the fire and passed through the sage smoke, after David anointed them with holy water and Charles painted them with pomegranate juice, the boys resumed their song. The noise of individual voices swelled to one sound—*earth my body, water my blood, air my breath, and fire my spirit*—so that Jean could not hear himself. David told them they were passing from this stage to the next and that tonight was a hinterland. But as Jean stands in the moonlight and recovers his breath, the warm, dark air filling his lungs, he does not feel changed. He is the same as he has always been, as he was with Kelly, as he will forever be. That is why he fled from Sandra.

He finds a flat rock and angles his body parallel to the smooth water, then flings the stone. It lands with a heavy plop. He tries again, and again he fails. But on the fifth go, it jumps twice. By the twentieth, it dances.

Is it the noise of the pebbles—picking them up, throwing them—or is it the memory of what Sandra whispered in his ear that distracts him, meaning he does not notice Tom's approach until the foliage next to him shakes and the other boy is standing there. Jean blinks stupidly, waiting for Tom to say something, waiting for Millie to appear behind him, but Tom says nothing, and Millie doesn't emerge, and so Jean says:

Where is she?

The girls went home. David caught them drinking.

Jean throws a stone. It sinks.

You need to flick. Here, try this one.

Jean tests the weight of the stone and runs his thumb along the rough surface. Like skin, he thinks, and as he flicks outward, he thinks, like a knife.

There you go.

Why is Tom here? Did he follow Jean, did he know Jean would be here? It is dark and Jean cannot see Tom's face properly.

Tom lowers himself onto the grass. Have you—

It is not how Jean imagined. This reunion. He thought that either they would fight or they would say sorry. His body is primed for it, but Tom seems easy, unhurried, leaning on his elbows and looking at the lake. Jean opens his tin. Tom is always easy and unhurried, walking around the school as if he owns it, hitting Jean on the back, the arm, the shoulder, as if it means nothing, because, Jean realises, it does mean nothing.

Hence why this easy slip into the patter of conversation, Tom chatting casually about the night's events. The lines between reality and magic, hate and love, yin and yang are thin, but only if you care. Only if, like Jean, you are driven uncontrollably by a desire so strong it stops you from sleeping. But if you are like Tom, walking through life unfazed, then there are no binaries in the first place. There is no hate and there is no love. Jean is not Tom's enemy, nor is he his lover.

Tom is still in his skirt, but he has a shirt on now. Jean lights the joint. Tom continues to talk—about the food, the cake, the fire, how he thought they were good onstage but could have been better, and about Charles.

He was fucked, did you see?

After Jean left the party, he found Charles rolling on the grass, cackling. The older man told Jean that *Perthro*, the symbol on Jean's rune, does not really mean *destiny*. It is special because scholars do not know what it means. For some it signifies a loss of faith, for others it simply means *nothing*. Charles talked quickly, excited by his own words, and Jean realised he was on something far stronger than nocino. He walked away from Charles then, but now he infers the full significance of Charles's silly factoid: Jean is not Tom's enemy, nor is he his lover; Jean is nothing.

All that nonce-juice, Tom says and when Jean doesn't respond, Tom continues, talking again about the food and the runes and whether Jean believes any of that bullshit, but leaving no room for Jean to respond. Jean sinks lower into his mood, letting Tom babble over him because he is not here; he is just a tin with some weed that Tom wants. Tom talks and talks: about how one year, before Jean's time, they killed the pig on the front lawn just as a local reporter arrived. He turned the car straight back around. You should have seen his face, smelt the burning rubber. The council threatened to close the school. Tom talks about Salome the pig and how he heard David prepping her for the *big day*. Do you think he's barmy? Tom says. Talking to a pig. David wasn't just talking to Salome, he was reading her the *Bible*. Which, you have to admit, is pretty fucking weird.

As Tom talks something shifts. Tom will not stop talking—and will Russia nuke us? Will we all die?—because Tom can't stop talking.

It is not the same as before. Tom is nervous.

Jean takes the burning end of the joint and holds it. Tom is nervous. The thought makes him snort.

What's so funny?

Nothing.

Tom is silent at last. He lobs a stone into the water. I hate it.

What?

People laughing.

I wasn't laughing at you.

When I was younger, Tom says quickly, as if he is confessing something, My dad made George and me race. But George is bigger and I had my fits, so . . . He laughed when I lost.

When was I laughing at you?

Tom groans and leans back. He covers his face, says in a rush and through his fingers: When Hugo said that thing.

When Jean realises what Tom is referring to—Hugo calling Tom a virgin—Jean almost laughs again. Jean fingers the glowing joint, takes another hit.

You've got nothing to worry about.

The air between them thickens. Jean cannot inhale, and the smoke leaves him in ragged breaths.

Sandra was looking for you.

Whatever.

Tom lets out a low whistle. Cold-hearted Blondie.

Jean's heart slides into his throat.

Got something better in London?

Jean flushes and is thankful for the dark.

What about Millie? Jean says.

She was begging for it, that's for sure.

So what's the problem?

Side by side, facing the lake, their knees almost touch. As Tom takes the end of the joint from Jean, their fingers catch; no, Tom hooks Jean's fingers, pressing the burning joint into Jean's palm. Jean gasps, the pain sharp and hot.

There is no problem, Tom says as he guides Jean's hand backward, twisting so Jean is forced to move with it, to the ground. Jean's mouth is dry, but Tom's is warm and hot—like Sandra's but also somehow like Millie's. I am kissing Millie, Jean thinks, and lets Tom push him to the ground.

The hinterland of the night stretches between them, and Jean lets Tom guide his hand to where he can feel, through the folds of Tom's skirt, that Tom is hard. He lets Tom peel away his clothes, stripping him of shirt, shorts, underwear, and shoes, each piece swiftly and gently removed as if Jean is a knot being undone.

After this, the nights will never be as long.

Tom rises above him, pulling his own shirt over his head, sliding off his skirt, and crouching above Jean, a knee on each side of his face. Jean takes Tom, spit slipping between his lips and sliding down his chin. Tom tastes sour and salty and as Jean moves his head, he is hit by the smell. It makes Jean gag, but he does not stop. He moves faster. Fuck, Tom says and twists so that his mouth is on Jean too.

Jean inadvertently buckles; this is new. This feeling of reciprocated pleasure that radiates from his centre, through his legs. He is silent; he does not moan or gasp or groan, and wonders if he should, startled and nervous that he is doing it, receiving it, wrong. Jean copies Tom, the way he moves, the way he uses his hand, and they move like this, one below, the other above. They glow in the moonlight, two boys in the dark. All thoughts fall away and Jean is overwhelmed by the hot, wet pleasure that is Tom's mouth, until a lone phrase remains: I am nothing. I am nothing.

VII

IT IS ALL OVER SCHOOL. BOYS WHISPERING ABOUT IT. IT IS THE biggest thing that has happened since that boy flung himself from the school roof two years ago. Eyes flicker, the creeping smile of scandal behind them. Jean keeps his head down and avoids contact, but still, he hears the comments. Like a curse it is passed around from sticky mouth to sticky ear. Jean hears from Samuel, who heard from Hugo, who got it straight from Tom.

Tom's brother, George, while driving back from a night on the town, skidded off the road, flipped his MG Convertible, and died.

It is the day after the solstice and the boys sit in Charles's classroom. The teacher, shades on, rabbit in lap, is perfectly still. Around them, the detritus of yesterday—yarn, twine, leaves, branches, glue, paint, feathers. Jean lost his headdress at some point last night and he wants to know with a fierceness that surprises him where it is. Is it in the hall or is it, shamefully, in the clearing? Is Tom's headdress there also, the feathers matted together, the fruit squashed.

The boys have already forgotten the task in hand. Or is it that Charles forgot to set one? Tom's seat is empty. Colin is carving something into the skirting board by the door. Theo is trying to give Percy a stick-and-poke tattoo. Charles lights a cigarette and the rabbit's nose twitches. The smoke is thick and cloying and makes Jean feel sick. There is a dull, repetitive ache in his brain, his mouth is dry, and his body is heavy. Too much nocino, not enough sleep.

Tom flipped Matron's Austin last year during the summer break. The holidays are famously best at Compton Manor with a loosening of rules and an absence of lessons: trips to the village, nights in the local pub, fires in the woods, days by the sea. The only problem is transport, which was why Tom and Hugo had taken to using Matron's car. Tom claims that Hugo was driving and vice versa. Whoever it was bombed through the fields at an ungodly speed, hit a fence, flipped the car, and landed upside down in a ditch. They emerged with only a few cuts and mild concussions. Once the car was hauled out, it was almost completely fine.

That wasn't the case for George though, was it?

Jean pictures the glass shattering, the metal crumpling, the car flipping; he tries to hold it in his mind, spinning continuously, staving off the inevitable. He has never met George, but from Tom's description, he imagines a man with a large forehead and a broad nose. Big hands that clench the wheel, trying to steer even though he is upside down.

Charles lets his cigarette burn without smoking it. Hugo,

pale and sweating, puts his head on the table. The room is close and dank. The methodical scrape and chip from where Colin is carving.

Jean has never known someone who died. There are his grandparents, but they died before he was born and remain shadowy, unknown figures in his mind. Rosa doesn't like to talk about them. He knows that she got on a train when she was sixteen and never saw them again. Never saw her home city, Berlin, or country, Germany, either. He knows his grandfather was sent to a camp, which one he's not sure, and that his grandmother found her way to Switzerland, where she spent her remaining years convalescing in a spa.

Other things he knows: His grandfather had dark hair and won an Iron Cross in the First World War. His wife was blonde and twenty-five years his junior. He came from Hungary, she from Ukraine, although, of course, neither country existed back then. He liked to play chess and listen to Wagner; she enjoyed parties and breaking plates. Him, Rosa loved; her, Rosa feared. These are the scraps Rosa has fed Jean over the years, offhand, almost to herself. Or, more often, he has learned them from Dinah on the nights when Rosa has passed out and, Dinah, putting Jean to bed, told him stories from his past. But there is so much he does not know. The quality of his grandparents' voices, the ways they moved across a room, their humour.

When he was seven, he asked Rosa what they were like. Rosa was in her studio, staring at her canvas. Her jacket was open and flecks of white paint dotted the black cotton dress underneath. Jean tried again. Again, she ignored him. The third time, he stamped his foot. It was swift the way Rosa jumped off the stool and grabbed his wrist. Usually when she was angry, she got red and pug-like, but this was different; her jaw was tight, her face blanched green, and her voice a whisper when she said, Jean, I am busy.

Then there are others who are still alive but who do not exist for him. Like his father and his uncle. Rosa's silence about these men is different. Inconsistent. Perforated by the small reminiscences, the deep grievances. His father left them, he knows, but as far as he can tell, the only thing his uncle did wrong was misunderstand art. He was industrial rather than aesthetic: He devoted his life to developing automatic knitting machines, he changed his last name to sound more English, he thought Rembrandt was depressing, he ate white bread and listened to Sinatra, and he had a small yappy dog. Rosa listed these things as evidence not only of her brother's lack of taste, but something more. Some moral deficiency in him with which she could not reconcile. As if, in these, Rosa's brother betrayed her very existence. To talk to him, then, was a kind of violence. When Rosa and he were teenagers, they were not friends, and now they are adults, they are strangers.

These absences work within Jean like termites, leaving tunnels in their wake. Jean is almost jealous of Tom because death is, in some ways, solid. The conversations and the arguments, the laughter, the pints, the trips to the sea, the wind in an open-top MG convertible.

Rosa would say: Bullshit. After death there is nothing. Your body goes into the ground. Bruce Lee has a different theory: Humans and nature are already in contact. When we die, our bodies may be eaten, but our spirits remain intact, feeding new life systems. That is literally what worm feed is. We return again and again and again. Like the car spinning in Jean's mind.

A chimney of ash builds along Charles's cigarette. Hugo runs out of the room holding his stomach. The car continues to revolve, hanging, suspended.

Some say Bruce was killed by gangsters, others that he was poisoned, and a small few that he died while having sex with his mistress. The official reason of death was swelling in the brain. Jean does not like this, reducing Bruce to the mere physical.

Charles's head sinks to his chest and the cigarette falls to the floor. Jean picks it up from where it begins to smoulder. He smokes out the window into the hot, static air.

When Jean saw Tom earlier today, face pale, being led down the corridor by David, he wanted to tell Tom that, although it sounds stupid, death is not the end. All he has to do is look around him: the reeds, the lake, the fish, the frogs, the leaves, the grass. These are signs, if you know how to read them properly. Bruce Lee died, technically, on 20 July 1973. Jean was with Kelly on the sixth floor of Biba where the Hare Krishna buffet is and where you can eat as much as you like, for free.

After, Jean showed Kelly the flamingos on the roof garden. How'd they get up here? she asked. Just then, one of the long, pink birds extended her wings, all three feet of them, and lifted into the sky. Her long neck made longer; her thin legs drawn together. As she glided over them, her shadow cast them in darkness and Jean could see that the undersides of her wings were not pink, but black. Their wings are clipped, Jean said, So they don't fly away. If that wasn't a sign that Bruce was still with them, he didn't know what was. This is what Jean wanted to say to Tom in the corridor earlier today, but then Tom looked through him, and Jean thought better of telling Tom that his dead brother was now, probably, a frog.

What? Charles mutters, jerking upright.

From where he sits at the window, Jean can see the bright red circle on Percy's skin. Colin continues to chip away at the floor. Charles looks around, dazed. He taps his chest and retrieves another cigarette. Lights it.

As you were.

Where are Charles's diatribes on poetry today? Last night, he was their friend, topping up their drinks and telling them to become men. But now, when they need him, he is not here. Jean cannot do it alone. He cannot hold this car, spinning in midair forever.

As they leave the classroom, the boredom and heat becoming too much, Charles mumbles something about exams. No one is listening. George is dead and there cannot be anything less important than poetry. Outside the room, the boys gather around Percy, checking out his new tattoo. There, in red and black, is an Ouroboros.

Later that day, David drives his Land Rover, on top of which is strapped the carcass of a cow, to the farm. The older boys are responsible for butchering it, as they must do, once a month. It is Jean and Colin's turn. Jean stands before the headless, flayed animal that not so long ago would have been standing, chewing cud. David is adamant that, even though they can't slaughter on school premises, the boys know the process.

First, the animal is taken to a chamber and stunned, most likely with gas. Its throat is cut so the blood rushes out and she dies as fast as possible.

After, the skin is removed, a tricky and skilled business. She is turned on her back, her forefeet and shanks (at the knee) dismembered by sliding a knife into the flat joints, the hind feet and shanks by sawing. The skin at her belly is sliced open in one clean motion, as is the skin by her hind legs. Next begins the difficult process of sliding. A knife is inserted where her belly is cut, and the hide is grabbed and pulled upward as the knife cuts in flat, straight strokes. The breastbone will need to be sawn in two and, if she is an old cow, so will the pelvis.

Remember the labour that goes into this, David said. The hide does not skin itself; it is removed with effort and skill by men. This huge, beautiful beast, at the hands of silly men. The hide is taken to more men who begin the stinking process of tanning. If the animal is male, the penis is removed before the flaying begins.

Now the carcass is ready to be hung. Lifted by her two hind legs and suspended from hooks on the wall.

Next, the gutting. The bung, otherwise known as the appendix, is removed by cutting around it and pulling it through the cavity at the base of the pelvis. When David told them this, Jean imagined a baby being born; now George's body busted open comes to mind. The bung can be used for many things, including mortadella, David's favourite ham. As the bung is pulled out, so come the intestines, otherwise known as tripe, also a favourite delicacy of the headmaster. The bung is snipped away and after the ligaments are cut, the intestines fall into a bucket, or failing that, onto the ground. The large, rich, brown liver is removed. Beef heart is delicious, Jean has been told, but lungs are a more acquired taste, reserved for the Scots.

Finally, the beast is beheaded. The tongue, of course, is kept. Sometimes the brains.

She hangs there, legs splayed, meat shiny and pink, for anywhere between a week and a month. Thick whorls of fat give shape and definition to her contours, revealing a preference for what kind of food, what kind of pasture, what shitting and fucking. The blood drips until there is nothing left, and still, she hangs by her feet, face to the ground. The flavour intensifying. Some people prefer ageing the meat while the hide is still on, but this is how David was taught.

The carcass is split into two sides, and this is how it arrives at the school. After hours of work, hundreds of different strokes with a knife, larger and smaller manoeuvres that cut, saw, trim, and otherwise reduce the animal to the meat. There is a Rembrandt painting of a dead cow that Rosa showed Jean. In it, the dark, rich reds and creamy hues of the carcass are illuminated by a single lamp in the corner of a barn. When Jean first saw it, it made his insides feel funny. But now that he knows the process, it seems like the carcass is quite far away from death. The carcass is a neat, painterly version.

Jean helps Colin shift the two sides onto the bench in the barn where the butchering happens. Colin is already trimming pieces of excess fat, moving quickly around his side.

A side breaks down into several cuts: neck and clod, chuck and blade, thick rib, thin rib, fore rib, shin, brisket, sirloin, flank, rump, silverside, topside, thick flank, and leg. Words that form a kind of poem in Jean's mind. First, he must divide the carcass into four sections. He needs to get a move on; Colin has already sliced through the chuck and is beginning to break up the ribs. As Jean slides the knife into the thick flesh, he is reminded of Tom's chest, the ribs visible through his skin. How they expanded and contracted with each breath. He separates the chuck from the ribs, the loin from the round, the flesh resistant at first, then yielding, and he is reminded of Tom's legs, how they intertwined with his, and how, after the cow is killed, its forelegs are pumped to remove excess blood.

Jean, David's voice cuts through his thoughts. Concentrate.

Colin is dividing the larger sections into their smaller cuts. Jean slides his knife into the leg joint, remembering how Tom slid his hand between Jean's legs and reached underneath his bollocks to find an opening. Pop, something burst inside him. How he had wriggled away from Tom's grasping hand because it had been so intense, instead offering his own hand as a temporary hole. He slices away the rump, the thick flank, and the leg. He is still behind Colin but at least he has some meat to show for it. Next, he attacks the sirloin with the same fervour with which Tom had attacked his hand, thrusting with his eyes closed, his hands around Jean's buttocks, pressing him closer, until—

Jean! David says, and Jean jumps back from the carcass, out of which the broken blade sticks, blood pooling.

Around the bone, not through it, David says. How many times have we done this?

Sorry. Jean bends to look at the damage and to hide his semi.

Love, David says. You must treat it with love.

The meat is mangled, the bone split, the knife bent. Part of the carcass hanging where the knife sticks out falls to the floor.

Yesterday, Tom cried out, a kind of strangled yelp, and a stone fell through Jean. Was that when George's car sped around the bend, skidding on the road and sailing over the hedgerow? Was it when the cow was being led into the chamber, when the animal was stunned, or when its throat was cut? Or was it when the car hit the bank on the other side, or when it flipped not once, not twice, but six times along the field, or was it when George's head slammed repeatedly into the windshield, the glass driving into his eyeballs, his brain? Was it when she was strung up and her head hacked off, falling with a thud and a squelch to the floor?

When Jean had just arrived at Compton Manor and was still in his phase of punching walls, he spent a lot of time in the sick bay, a bloodied bandage around his fist. Often, he was alone; sometimes, others joined him. Usually, he did not talk to them, but one day a boy asked him for a cigarette. Jean was struck by his manner: until then, boys had stuck their noses up at Jean, but this one seemed nice, friendly even. Jean couldn't tell why he was there; he didn't seem hurt, but Jean did not ask. They smoked together, the boy by the window, Jean in the ratty armchair on the other side of the room. Then the boy left. A few minutes later: a whip of air and a crack, something heavy and dense and full of stuff hitting the gravel. The boy's half-smoked cigarette still burning in the ashtray.

So, Jean has known someone who died.

VIII

HELLO DARLING. HELLO?

Hi.

It's good to hear your voice.

How have you been?

Yeah.

God it's good to hear your voice. Wait one sec, someone's at the door. Stay there. Don't move, OK? OK?

OK.

Don't go anywhere.

OK.

Don't.

Rosa.

Hello? Jean?

Yes—

Hello?

I'm here.

It was a salesman. You know their type, with the mops and the buckets and the gloves and the endless sponges. The way they present them, like they're unbelievably valuable—diamonds or some fantastically naughty thing you can't get in the regular shops. Porn! Nothing like the fishman. Jerry. He is so bloody rude. You used to do this fantastic impression. How did it go: I'm Jerry, fuck off—

He doesn't sound like that.

Fuck off, I'm Jerry.

Hello, I'm Jerry. Have a terrible morning and an awful fucking life.

That's it!

Fish for sale but not for you, you bloody git.

His funny little high voice!

Yes, madam, I do have sole, but it's burning in hell.

Oh God—

You hate plaice? Yes, you do live in a shithole.

Too good, I'm going to—

Used to hate shellfish, too, until I became a prawn again Christian.

—wet myself.

Why do you bother?

God knows. I buy bloody everything. Last week I bought

half the truck, had to freeze most of it. But he did have scallops. That will be nice won't it, when you're back, scallops in the garden?

Does he still wear those trousers?

God yes.

With the—

Hideous.

And the blood—

You can smell him a mile away.

Gross.

Nothing like the cloth man. Clean as a whistle. And very enthusiastic. Still I end up buying something just to get rid of him. It happened to me just now.

Oh no.

I know!

They see you coming from a mile away.

I know.

Next time shut the door in his face.

I needed you here! I needed my son to save me from the cloth man.

Save you from yourself.

Exactly.

Did he tell you about his starving kids at home?

Don't.

No way.

Oh God.

That's the oldest trick in the book.

Children.

What?

It's children not kids. Horrid Americanism.

And you fell for it.

I told him I couldn't talk because I had my son on the phone, waiting—

Jesus.

And then he starts talking about his son. Once he was onto little Jimmy, he wouldn't stop. How he's starting big school in the autumn, he's so excited, but isn't the uniform expensive, and the travel fare, and—

Oh God—

No, he was serious, Jean, I really believed him.

Of course you did.

Although now that you say it, he did seem a bit young to have an eleven-year-old boy.

How much did you buy?

I don't want to talk about it.

Oh dear.

Just some cloths.

Rosa.

And maybe some matching tea towels. And a bucket and a mop. And some strange sponges that are meant to be very good for grease, and, Oh God, what an ass!

Silly.

It's because I was desperate to get back to the phone. This is what happens when you're away, Jean. I spend all my money on cleaning products and fish. I need you to come home!

You got screwed.

All to get back to my darling son, who I know loves to talk to me so much.

You shouldn't have.

I'm screwed either way, whether they want to sell me something or not. I should have a sign: "Mad woman, will buy anything."

I think you already do.

The worst part is he was Northern. I mean I should have known it was a stitch up. What's it you say, anything north of Watford is—

I don't say that anymore.

Is abroad!

I've got a friend from the north.

And he had this greasy hair, and this voice so thick you could barely—

Are they fishy?

What?

Scallops.

They're fish.

Are they fishy?

Shellfish, technically.

I don't like them.

Don't be ridiculous.

I don't.

They're delicious. You'll love them.

Can you promise?

I must remember to take the salmon out of the freezer. Dinah is coming round later. Don't let me forget.

Can you promise?

Oh Jean.

Nah.

I'm not doing this. What's happened? What did I say? We were having such a nice time.

I hate them.

You can't possibly hate them.

I do.

They were very expensive.

I've got to go.

Jean, come on.

I'm going camping.

Let's not ruin this.

I've got to—

Camping? When?

Tomorrow. All the last years do it.

What about exams?

It's David's idea.

Where? For how long?

Rosa.

Who will be with you?

It's all sorted.

Is it safe?

Rosa.

Jean, there are a lot of fucked-up people—

I have to go now.

Tell me how you are.

I'm fine.

Three things.

I jumped over a fire.

You did what?

I, using my two legs, jumped. Over. A. Fire.

What's going on over there? What have you been studying?

Dunno.

Do not, Jean. You do not know. Do not be a slob.

I do not giveth a shitteth.

Oh Jean. Maybe this was the wrong—

Couple-colour as a brinded cow.

Couple, what?

Rose-moles. Finches' wings.

I see.

Whatever is fickle, freckled (who knows how?).

Now you're being an ass.

With swift, slow; sweet, sour; adazzle, dim:

You know exams are in two weeks.

Praise Him.

Can you write an essay?

I need—

Are you learning anything useful?

—to go.

You're the one who needs these.

Yesterday I cut up a cow.

Christ.

Painted our faces with blood and ran naked through the woods.

This isn't a joke, Jean.

Smeared shit on the trees.

I give up!

And tried to eat our own toes, like the spastics we are.

Who is your new friend?

What?

You said you had a friend from the north.

No, I didn't.

Will I get to meet him?

No.

I'd like to.

I didn't say that.

You could invite him to stay.

Shut up.

It's just you've never had anyone to stay, and it might be nice for you.

Fucking hell.

There's no need to jump down my throat. If you want. It's there.

Why do you never just shut up?

Jean . . . I just want to talk with you, Jean.

Talk then.

It's called a conversation; it involves both of us.

Blah, blah, blah, blah.

You can be a real shit you know that?

Here she is.

When you're home this summer, you're getting a job. I'm certainly not supporting you—

I'm not coming back.

What?

I'm not.

And where will you go?

China.

China! Ha, yes, by all means, go to China.

It's always the mother's fault.

Rosa.

Everything. Blame the mother, go on.

Rosa.

I can't do anything right.

Rosa.

Nobody loves me.

Rosa.

No one has ever loved me.

Just stop.

I'm alone.

Fuck's sake.

Don't swear.

Stop being a fucking bitch then.

Jean.

You are.

You won't even tell me the name of your friend.

I don't have any friends.

Oh darling.

Shut up—

Sweetie, I'm sure lots of people—

Shut the fuck up. Shut up. Shut up. Fuck.

Jean, you need to calm down.

You're fucking pathetic, do you know that?

Deep breaths.

You don't even have a job.

Jean.

Painting isn't a job. Waving a brush around with your bitch friends.

Jean.

Drawing pictures. What the fuck is that? It's sick, that's what it is. I feel fucking sorry for you. You're sick and sad and you've got fucking problems.

What is this about Jean? What's going on?

Jean.

Jean?

IX

JEAN HAS BEEN WALKING FOR THREE HOURS NOW. IT IS NOT YET eight o'clock, but the sun is hot and high in the sky. He has kept a good pace and, despite a few wrong turns and an intimidating interaction with some sheep, he should reach his destination by suppertime.

Each last-year boy spends three days and three nights in the *wilderness* alone, building his shelter, cooking his food over a fire, and being with nature (shitting in a hole, Hugo says). Not only are they learning survival skills, says David, but they are learning more about themselves. Part of the hike is the night vigil, where, on the final night, the boys are encouraged to stay awake—by firelight or, for the truly brave, in the darkness—reflecting on all that has been and all that is yet to come. Those who come back having done so have a strange look in their eyes, walk a little taller, move with more grace. I am changed, they say.

The night before they left, Jean couldn't sleep. Tom, who returned to school after only four days at home, found Jean checking his pack and studying his map in the billiard room.

Tom was paler than usual, his face drawn and closed. Jean wanted to ask him how the funeral was, how he was, but the way Tom sat down and jumped up, pacing the room and asking in a quick, manic voice what Jean was taking, where he was going, stopped Jean from bringing up George's death. To the sea, Jean said, eyeing Tom warily from the floor. Most boys had decided to head east into the weald or west for higher ground, but Jean was choosing to do a gruelling twenty-seven miles on his first day so he could spend the next two on the beach, swimming, resting, before hiking back.

Cool, Tom said, crouching down, his knees brushing against Jean's. I think I'll go to the sea too.

Tom concentrated on the map. He seemed fragile in the dim light of the room. The lines of his cheekbones and jaw gave Jean the impression that his face had been broken and glued back together. Jean wanted to stroke Tom's cheek, to cup his face, but when he shifted, Tom tensed. He looked stricken, as if, were Jean to touch him, he would break apart again.

Tom stood, talking loudly and confidently about the route he would take, and Jean wondered if he had imagined the invitation. Tom didn't look sad at all. Didn't look like his brother had just died.

As Jean reclines against a mossy mound now, he imagines Tom striding along, arms tense with the weight of his pack, sweat pooling at his pits and across his chest. Around his groin. The dank smell of Tom the night of summer solstice. Jean almost gagged as Tom hovered above him. But as he took Tom in his mouth, he was surprised by the taste. Sharp, yes, and salty, but also sweet.

Jean drinks from his metal canteen, enjoying the shock of cold water down his gullet. He should get going. He has seven hours of walking ahead of him if he keeps pace, nine if he slows. In the dark of the billiard room, Tom had pointed casually to the field where he would end up, where Jean could find him, if he wanted. Jean checks the coordinates on the map. A single field, about a mile from the nearest farm, with a stream running through it. A copse, too, which will be useful when they build a fire. Jean has been collecting kindling as he walks for this very purpose. So far, he has some sheep's wool and cherry bark. He fingers the soft wool in his pocket. His sweat has started to cool and his limbs feel stiff. Better get a move on.

After Tom and Jean studied the map together, they went outside to smoke. They didn't talk and Tom took concentrated, deep drags of the joint. He looked at Jean with red-rimmed eyes, as if searching for him through a fog.

Don't be scared, Blondie, Tom said, his sour breath close. He thrust a hand on Jean's shoulder, and Jean realised that Tom thought Jean couldn't sleep for this reason. Don't be scared.

But Jean is not afraid of the wilderness. He knows how to survive. He knows how to light a fire from flint and steel, holding both close so the sparks catch quickly. He knows how to forage for herbs from holidays with Rosa, her walking ahead, pointing to shrubs, and calling out their names. He has collected St. John's wort today. Tricky to identify because it is similar in growth and appearance to the nonedible ragwort. Crushing the petals between his fingers, the telltale crimson oil spreads across them. It is good for bruises and bumps. The hedgerows are fragrant with elderflower. David will be collecting the frothy white buds to make his famous cordial; Charles to brew champagne. The scene comforted Jean as he wandered down unknown paths, hard and uneven where the mud, bruised by the prints of men and animals, had dried. Scientists say it has been the driest summer in years and pray for rain; the earth is burning, they say, the earth will end.

Jean did not tell this to Tom the night before; instead, he placed his own hand over Tom's and pressed it into his shoulder.

Nor did he tell Tom that he was excited. An excitement that caught in his throat.

Before Tom found him in the billiard room, Jean's earlier conversation with Rosa had been playing in his mind, her voice hammering into his skull. At the time he had wanted to slam the receiver into Rosa's head, but as he squatted in the billiard room, he realised it didn't matter. Because the next day he would be going on his hike. It was this thought that made it impossible to sleep.

For a long time, all Jean wanted was to be in the wilderness. All Jean wants, really, is to avoid the lines that dissect his life—like those that demarcate the land before him now—and tell him where he can and can't be. And as he replaces his canteen in the side of his pack, as he checks that all the straps are tied tightly, as he swings the bag onto his back, takes a last look at the map, and heads down the path that skirts the edge of the field lush with green furls, he feels like he is walking away not just from school, but from life. He feels like he is disappearing.

Of course he does not disappear. He is still a body with needs and wants and hunger. So hungry, as he pauses at the edge of a forest for lunch.

His map tells him that he is near a village called Three Cups Corner. England is filled with funny names: Dallington Forest, Warbleton, Little Sprats, Foul Mile, Stunt's Green, Ginger Green, Cowbeech. They sound like settings for outrageous escapades or naughty tricks; not clandestine meetings. Names that come straight out of the children's books that Rosa illustrated using his face.

He unwraps his sandwich: brown bread, cheese, pickle. He retrieves his Opinel—a birthday present from Dinah with the note, *You're not supposed to send knives in the post, but I won't tell if you don't!*—to cut a tomato. Each quarter bright red and juicy, spilling seeds onto his bare thigh.

That night on the solstice, Tom spun round and put *his* face between Jean's thighs. Jean did not disappear then. He felt fully in himself; felt, fully, the potential of what it could be like with Tom, the joy of mutual pleasure. The heat from the underside of Tom's bollocks hit him, along with the realisation that Tom was smelling, tasting the same. Tom didn't let Jean finish in his mouth, so Jean is still the only person who has tasted his own cum.

The bread of his sandwich is stale, and the cheese is sweaty. But the pickle is sharp and the tomato refreshing. He drinks more from his canteen, careful not to drink too much.

Yes, for a long time all Jean wanted was to be in the wilderness, a nonplace where he himself does not exist. But since Tom, this desire has been complicated. He would like, yes, to go somewhere he can feel the freedom of his own wants, but he'd also like Tom to be there. It is *this* thought that scares him. Because to be with Tom is to be so brazenly faced with himself. Jean knows he must exist in his own life as himself, his faults laid bare. He isn't sure yet how to do that. There is time to learn. Tonight, he can practice.

He cools off in a stream, dunking his head and wetting his T-shirt before tying it around his neck and hairline, the way Charles showed him, the way he had done in Afghanistan on the Silk Road. They way Jean and Tom will surely do when they go to China.

Silk Road, Trans-Siberian Railway, it is true that these names are better than Catsfield and Marlspit. But as Jean continues along the blissfully empty path toward an unmarked field on the map, emerging from the woods into another field, this time in brilliant gold, the hay waiting to be cut and turned into large rounds, he is surprised to find the lyrics of "Jerusalem" come to him. Now, finally, he remembers the lines.

The rest of the walk is harder. He gets lost somewhere around Ashburnham and doubles back. They are not meant to take roads, but Jean is faced with an electric fence or tarmac. He finds the bridleway and weaves through a series of small woods, crossing styles, skirting along fields, and climbing through hedgerows, brambles scraping his flesh, until finally he reaches the spot. Sweet Willow Wood. The stream runs to the north, wider than he imagined, almost a river, although he can see where it has dropped several feet from the drought. Here, the slight incline of the field, and there, the copse. The fence markers match the shape on his map. It is not directly on the coast but close enough.

The sores on Jean's shoulders are rubbed raw, his arms are scratched, and he has blisters on his feet. Before attending to these, he gathers wood for a large fire tonight and a small one tomorrow morning. He unpacks the food in his bag that needs to cool, wrapping bacon, butter, and a carton of milk in hessian, tying a rope, and lowering the parcel into the stream before attaching the other end to a tree. He pitches his tent, clicking together the A-frame efficiently and checking that the inner and outer linings are not touching—if the linings touch, the tent will be soaked by the morning dew, something he learned the hard way from years of summer holidays with Rosa.

Jean was responsible for setting up the tent while Rosa found whoever was in charge. He was good at it and would be done long before she came back; often wandering through the campsite to find her in the bar, half a bottle drunk. She would be talking to a man, French, Swiss, Italian (never German), bangles sliding wildly up and down her arms. When she saw Jean, she would squish his face between her palms, saying, Look at my gorgeous boy. Jean untangled himself and, while she poured another glass, her torso stiffly swaying, the man slipped away. Rosa then spent the rest of the evening with her head on Jean's shoulder, the tears slipping freely down her cheeks and soaking his shirt. She blew her nose on her sleeve and whispered, My gorgeous, gorgeous boy. Occasionally she got lucky and Jean slept in the tent alone. Worse were the men who perked up when they saw Jean. Who looked at him with hungry eyes.

Yes, Jean has been learning to survive for years.

He turfs a pit and lays two logs parallel inside it. Next, he nestles the sheep's wool and cherry bark and stacks the kindling tightly enough so that the twigs—thinner than matchsticks—don't come apart, but not so tight that the oxygen is cut off. He takes the flint and steel that David gave him and positions himself. He would like, if he can, not to use the paraffin. He points the flint bar at a forty-five-degree angle and strikes once, hard, along its shaft. Nothing. He strikes again and this time a few sparks escape, but they land nowhere. He strikes again, and again his sparks refuse to jump from flint to wool.

When he first came to Compton Manor, there was the fire test. They were given only three matches. Jean had never made a fire before; OK, he had made a fire, but using dry, nail-studded wood in a bin round the back of a car park, the varnish emitting a caustic scent that burned his nostrils, or pouring petrol on a barn door, the night sky turned Day-Glo from the flames. He didn't know that you had to dig a pit so you didn't scorch the earth. He didn't know that you should spend most of your time collecting wood and that the wood should be of different sizes, from twig to log, and that the actual lighting of the fire, the striking part, came at the very end of this methodical preparation. He'd wasted his three matches by trying to light a moss-covered branch. The feeling of humiliation as he watched small fires spring up around him, boys' faces illuminated, while he remained cold and dark.

He tugs a piece of wool loose so it is bare to the flame. Then he strikes again and this time the spark leaps, like magic, from his fingers. During the fire test, he had kicked his pile of wood and stormed off so no one would see him crying. He is glad, now, that he did not use his paraffin.

As the fire eats the skinny wood, he feeds it more, placing the branches delicately onto the steadily leaping flame.

Once the fire is established, with thick logs glowing white, orange, pink and blue, he fills his billy tin from the stream and boils water. He adds the St. John's wort, the yellow flowers crumpling in the steam and releasing their crimson nectar. Once the poultice is made, he rubs it along his shoulders and on his ankles, smarting at the sting.

All there is to do is wait. It is evening. He is in a beautiful field, alone, with nothing to do and no one to bother him. But he is on edge. Sensitive to the smallest noise. He rehearses what he will say; how he will describe his walk, the empty fields, the blue sky, the heat. The single old man with an eye patch on the road from Dallington who was walking a cow. He seemed from a different world in his handmade clothes and boots. As if he had walked straight out of the ancient times that David loves to talk about. Jean raised a hand but the man continued walking, the cow moving with lumbering grace beside him, as if he did not see Jean. As if their two worlds were merely passing each other for a fraction of a second, like two trains aligning in a tunnel, the glow of the other carriage an uncanny, bright mirror, before being swallowed by darkness. When Jean turned back, the man and cow had disappeared.

Or he will tell Tom about his blisters and how he has treated them with his own poultice. Witch, Tom will call him. Or they won't speak at all, and the first thing Tom will do is grab the back of Jean's hair and crush his face. Jean gets hard thinking about it.

He heats a tin of baked beans in another billy tin and toasts bread on a stick. He wants bacon but decides to save it for the morning. He dips the hot bread, crisp and burnt on the edges, into the pot of beans. For a while he stays like this, crouched by the fire. The food makes him feel better but also somehow worse, leaving the dull ache of disappointment.

The fire has settled into glowing embers, the sky dark, punctured with stars. Jean scatters the embers. He wants them to remain warm but refrain from lighting the dry grass. He unrolls his sleeping bag, deciding it is warm enough to sleep outside, deciding he can't be bothered to wash up or to brush his teeth, and climbs in.

When Jean wakes the following morning, his first thought is that he did not spread the fire enough and the field is aflame, but as he coughs and blinks away the smoke, he sees that the fire is perfectly contained within its pit, and that by it, is Tom. Tom lays four strands of bacon into a pan; they shrink and spit as they touch the heat. Jean watches Tom watching the bacon, the pan, the fire for a minute. There are dark circles around his eyes and the top of his nose is burnt. He is crouching, staring at the flames. When Tom sees that Jean is awake his face hardens, and he chucks him a loaf of bread. It hits Jean in the chest, and he fumbles, almost dropping it in the dirt.

When—

Last night.

Tom has not pitched his tent. He must have slept next to Jean.

The fridge was in the sun this morning, Tom says.

Yesterday, when Jean sank the hessian sack into the stream, it wasn't in the sun. But, of course, the sun moves.

You going to cut that? Tom says, gesturing at the loaf.

Jean's body is aching and stiff from where he slept on the hard ground, his mouth stale and fuzzy. He is moving slowly, and he can feel Tom's impatience; while Jean looks for his knife, Tom chucks him his own.

I've got tea.

I forgot to get water.

Lucky one of us has brains. Tom nods to the gallon bottle next to him. Met the farmer too.

David has two rules: 1) Always ask permission before you camp, 2) leave no trace. Borrowed, he told the boys as they stomped their feet in the dawn, from native tribes who moved through the country. Who did not consider the land to be theirs, anyone's. Jean meant to go to the farm, he meant to fill up on water and ask permission to camp in the field. The problem in England is property. The bacon spits in the pan, the smell mixing with the smoke. Or more specifically, capitalism. In England men own land and to camp on it without permission is illegal. He blames, also, the man on the road with the cow. He could explain this to Tom—it wasn't my fault, it was the birth of Christianity and the destruction of common land—but Tom squints at him and Jean cannot tell if his face is pink from the fire or from irritation.

Tom makes the sandwiches while Jean makes the tea. The bread tastes smoky and burnt, the bacon salty and crisp. They have no sauce. It is the most delicious thing Jean has ever eaten. Tom smokes a cigarette, spitting on a burning log.

What time is it? Jean says, finally feeling more awake, but Tom, instead of answering, nudges a log with his boot, dislodging another, so that the smoke spreads, stinging Jean's eyes and forcing him to move.

Can't be later than seven, Jean tries again.

While Tom thought of the practical things like water and safety, what did Jean do? Is this the real reason Tom suggested, the night before they left, that they meet up on the hike—not because he wants to see Jean but because he thinks Jean can't cope? And is this why Tom isn't talking to him.

Tom throws the last of his tea on the fire; the hissing and the smoke increase. Don't look at me like that, he says. Then: Come on.

They walk to Bexhill, the closest town and, importantly, where the sea is. It is not far from where they have set up camp, but their limbs and backs are tired from yesterday's hike. Jean points out herbs, telling Tom their uses, trying, in some way, to redeem himself. To show he will not be useless when they are on the edge of a mountain in Russia. Before they left, Tom grimaced at the remains of Jean's poultice, but when Jean explained it was for blisters, Tom softened. Now Jean picks a long, green stem.

Try it.

Tom pulls his mouth into a comical show of disgust.

Go on.

What about dog piss?

Jean rips a bit and puts it in his mouth.

Or human piss?

Here.

Tom takes a tiny, suspicious bite. As he chews, his wrinkled nose stretches; he chews with longer, more relaxed movements and his eyes widen with astonishment.

Holy shit.

I told you.

What is that?

Three-cornered leek.

No, what's that flavour? Like—

Garlic.

Tom slaps Jean on the back, and even though it hurts Jean's blisters, he smiles.

Shit.

It is true that Tom can fish and hunt and shoot, that he knows about birds and frogs and rabbits, about apples and berries, but weeds? That you can eat? At the side of the road no less.

That's fucking amazing, Tom says. No, seriously that's class. Where'd you pick that up?

On holiday, Rosa would be up and ready, no matter how much she'd drunk the night before. Brewing coffee on their little gas stove, the morning mist rising around her. They would go for a walk, sometimes for three or four hours, through foreign fields, along coastal paths and dense pine forest. Rosa, wearing a swimsuit and linen shirt, straw hat casting a shadow across her face, would tug at the leaves. She spoke softly, naming each one like an old friend, what they were good for, what they weren't.

When he was little, she turned it into a game, crouching on the ground and spreading her palm wide to show him five different leaves. He would crouch too, holding on to her arm with his small hand, while she told him a story, pointing to each leaf in turn—here was a princess, here a prince, there an ogre, a wizard, and a magic potion—before snapping her fist closed, only a hint of green poking through her knuckles. Jean's challenge was to find each leaf, which he did by repeating the story to himself under his breath as he marched through the impossibly long grass. Once he had collected them, Rosa, now cross-legged on the ground, Jean slumped in her lap, went through them. Ash, blackthorn, fig, valerian, and Jean's favourite, Russian sage.

Things that thrived in the Mediterranean soil. Jean liked the way plants took on new identities, becoming characters that danced through his mind.

When he was older, she dropped the story part, but their best conversations, both on holiday and at home, are still about plants. Jean can name hundreds, in France and in England, their names etched on the insides of his eyelids. He knows things that even Rosa doesn't; Rosa, swelling with happy surprise when Jean identifies something she is not familiar with.

I don't know, Jean says now. He does not want to bring up Rosa. Or France.

Always so fucking mysterious, Blondie, Tom says as he slings an arm around Jean. The sun is directly above them, and their shadows are stubs by their feet. Tom is shorter than Jean and the angle of his arm means Jean can feel the dampness of his pit, smell it. Jean wraps his own arm around Tom, gripping the slope of shoulder where muscle meets bone. Their hips bump as they walk. Jean likes that, the feeling of bumping hips with Tom. As the first houses appear, however, Tom relinquishes him.

How old-fashioned the shop fronts seem compared with London's: the faded red of Owbridge's Lung Tonic at the chemist's made paler by sea salt and wind; the fishmongers' iridescent wares spilling onto the street; the sweet shop, rows of coloured jewels, some dusty, others clear.

Tom makes them buy groceries first, pooling their ration money. More bread, eggs, a tomato, and three bottles of ale. Tom does the talking, and Jean notices that he speaks like a southerner. Yes, they're camping just up the road. A Duke of Edinburgh sort of thing. They're from a school nearby. No, not that hippie one, terrible place. No somewhere else. St. Barnard's—Oh well it's very small and exclusive, you won't have heard of it but ta very much for the extra apple, growing boys and all that! Ta-ra now!

They buy a bag of chips, which they eat on the seafront. The chips are fat and fresh, and Jean burns his mouth eating so many at once.

How comes it doesn't look the same?

What?

That leek thing. Doesn't look like garlic. Or leek.

Jean pulls the crisp shell from a chip, revealing its fluffy centre.

It isn't.

How'd you mean?

Onion, leek, garlic, chives—

Chives?

They're related.

Tom takes a handful of chips and stuffs them in his mouth. His lips are shiny with grease. He is sitting next to Jean, and their legs are almost touching. Jean looks out at the beach: before him, bodies clad in brightly coloured swimming costumes packed tightly together. Children screaming. Parents yelling. Ice-cream vendors weaving between, calling out clearly above the rest. Mint Choc-chip. Lemon Sorbet. French Vanilla! A dog jumps to catch a Frisbee, spraying a young, tanned couple in sand. Beyond, the sea. Not the blue of the Mediterranean, but still, it sparkles.

Let's swim.

They fold their clothes over the groceries and race, in just their boxer shorts, into the water, striking out beyond the break. When Jean turns, the noises of the beach are muffled by the lapping of the sea. Tom treads water next to him, his hair glistening in the sun. Jean lies on his back and closes his eyes, the lapping filling his ears. When he opens his eyes again, it seems like Tom is closer. There are the freckles, the small scar above his eyebrow, the bloom of pink on his cheeks. He smiles, panting and breathless from keeping afloat.

After, they dry on the sand. Jean is startled when Tom removes his wet togs and goes commando in his denim cutoffs. Jean turns and changes more demurely. Not just because he is embarrassed but because he cannot stop thinking about Tom's smooth, white buttocks. They stroll along the promenade and Jean isn't sure, but it feels like they are walking closer. The tension and separation he felt at breakfast has evaporated in the sun. Has Tom forgiven him? Tom, whose forehead and nose are the colour of a ripe peach.

What? Tom says.

Nothing. What?

Tom's eyes flick to Jean's lips then back again. He reaches up and Jean finds himself leaning forward as Tom presses his thumb to the top part of Jean's lip.

Seaweed, Tom says.

They walk back to camp, their shadows stretched lazily in front. The journey is uphill, but it is not just the exertion that makes Jean's heartbeat quicken. As the houses are swapped for hedgerows and the stile appears up ahead, he is out of breath: eager and, also, reluctant. They walk in silence. Uncharacteristically, Tom has not touched Jean again—no friendly slap on the back, or arm around the shoulder—as if he, too, is unsure.

The walk across the field seems endless. Will they go into the tent or will Tom press Jean into the grass by the fire? Will they head for the woods where it is more sheltered? He would, if Tom reached out now, collapse onto the ground and give him everything. Tom strides ahead with purpose. When they arrive, he kneels by the fire and stacks wood; unpacks the groceries. Jean blinks back his disappointment. There is a lump in his throat.

You want to eat? I'm starving, Tom says.

Jean doesn't say that eating is the last thing on his mind. Now that they are alone, it is as if there is more distance between them. Or was it always like this, and did Jean imagine—what exactly? Tom's thumb pressing his lip.

By the time they have eaten and smoked two joints, Tom on the other side of the fire, asking Jean questions about what else is edible, and then, more interestingly, what is poisonous, Jean has given up hope. This wasn't part of his imagined plan: the first night he wasted by falling asleep, and Tom seems content to spend their second compiling a Britannica of English wild herbs. If Jean had known Tom would be such an eager student, he never would have told him about three-cornered leek.

Jean does not expect anything will happen, then, when Tom suggests a swim in the river. They are both still covered in salt from the sea and smoke and sweat from the fire. It is not yet dark, and it is still warm. When they get into the water, Jean is shocked by the cold and by Tom's nakedness. This time, he does not turn away.

At school there are communal showers and, usually, there is someone skidding nude down the corridor, another boy whipping him with a towel, but those bodies are accompanied by the noise and chaos of being a teenager. Jean has never seen Tom, all of him, like this. It is not just about his long, dark pink penis surrounded by curls. It is about his head, neck, back, thighs, arms, shins, ankles. Jean is aware, also, that this must be the first time Tom has seen him. He feels Tom take in his long, skinny arms, his concave chest, and his own penis, surrounded by pale hair. Does he feel the same about these things that Jean feels for the dip in Tom's collarbones? The soft part of his forearm.

Tom is pale from the cold. Jean is reminded of months earlier when David packed them into his Land Rover and drove them to Fishbourne Palace. In the centre the statue stood, buff marble mottled by lines of brown and blue, as Tom's skin is veined now. Jean moves toward Tom. The water is not so deep here, and Jean crouches low, creeping along the riverbed. Who was he?

Nero, Tom whips his head and flecks of water fall on Jean's face. Piece of work he was.

Yeah?

Tom dips lower into the water, and as his legs drift up, Jean catches them.

Didn't he do some fucked-up shit? Jean asks.

Jean half expects Tom to recoil, but Tom lets himself be pulled closer, his hands making ripples in the current.

He tried to kill his mum.

How?

Well, Tom says, slowly, First, he tried to poison her.

With what?

Tom is half sitting in the water, his legs loose around Jean's waist, his body upright, arms outstretched. Jean circles his arms around Tom's torso, feeling the muscles in Tom's back tense.

You're the witch.

Jean pretends to consider this, squinting at the sky.

I mean, it could be anything.

What would you use?

In ancient Rome?

Whenever.

When David said he was taking them to a palace, Jean had imagined a grand thing with pillars and domes. The underground cavern was a surprise. The floor extended into the dimness, dappled by faded tiles. As David stood in the gloom, he explained that what the boys could see was only a fraction of the original. The royal structure had been buried by time, bodies layered with other bodies and dirt and sewers and houses. The floor lights cast long, black shadows up David's face, hollowing his eyes and inverting the curve of his chin. Standing in the subterranean palace, Jean became aware for the first time of his own mortality; so now, the solidity of Tom's thighs around his hips, the ridge of spots on his back, the freezing water, make him feel alive.

Hemlock probably, Jean says.

There you go.

To be honest, it grows everywhere. I saw some earlier, up by the woods.

I should be careful then.

Tom's hands rest on Jean's hips lightly, then firmly. The water is shallower than the sea, and their legs scrape the bottom.

Very careful.

What does it look like?

Green stems. White flowers.

Helpful. Anyway, Tom says, It didn't work.

What happened?

He tried to crush her with a rock.

Now that the initial shock has passed, the cold reverses, and a glorious warmth radiates through Jean. Tom's erection presses against his thigh. A nightingale calls.

But that didn't work either, so he put her in a boat.

A boat?

Tom moves from one side of Jean's face to the other, lips brush lips. He grips Jean harder, pressing their bodies together, before whispering, A boat designed to sink, and tipping Jean backward.

Water rushes up Jean's nose as his balance is upturned. His breath is almost gone; he feels lightheaded. He thrashes against Tom but because of the way Tom has shifted his weight, so his feet are on the river floor but his legs are clamped around Jean's waist, Jean cannot break free. There is a pressure in his chest, simmering into hysteria. If he opens his eyes, he can see Tom's face above him; it is distorted through the warped fury of the water, like a carnival mirror.

What Jean had taken for a joke slips into something sharp. This feeling of being trapped and Tom's laughing image remind him of another time, another place. Provence last summer, almost a year ago. Rosa's latest new friend was a short man from central Rome (another Roman) who charmed her by discussing the terror of the Trevi Fountain at high season. The next day, this Italian bumped into Jean in the café where he was picking at an old croissant. Jean did not want to talk to him, he certainly did not want to play table tennis, but Rosa was off sketching and Jean did not feel he could say no when the man suggested a game.

Each time Jean scored, the man whacked Jean on the arse with his bat. Jean tried to lose but he had the impression that the man let him win. Sweat formed on the man's lip and his stomach strained against his brightly patterned shirt. Jean can't say why he stayed, letting the man slap him on the arse. Was it a sense of loyalty, or was it out of a sense of shame, or was it because he sensed what the man sensed in him? Because he wanted him to sense it. Something held him there, just as Tom holds him now, bubbles streaming past his eyes. Fuck, Jean doesn't want his last thoughts to be of that Italian man. But then Tom gives way, and the world is rushing up to meet Jean, and he emerges, screaming like a newborn.

You wanker, Jean coughs as he follows Tom onto the bank. The air makes his body feel on fire. Tom is laughing, the final rays casting him in a deep orange glow.

It didn't work, Tom says, holding up his hands in defence.

Jean sits on Tom, pinning his arms.

Nero's mum swam to shore.

Wanker.

You're telling me, Tom says. He struggles but Jean has him clamped between his thighs. Fucking sicko shagged his mum.

What?

Nero. He was fucking his mum.

What? Jean sits back, disgusted, and in this space, Tom flips him so it is Jean who is pinned to the ground. Jean kicks but his legs flail in open air.

Everyone was doing it, Tom leans closer. Men and women. Men and men.

The nightingale's song advances, the notes repeating and building on top of one another. Tom inches forward so their noses are pressed together. Jean is cold. The heat of the day is long past, and he is still wet. A shiver, starting in his sphincter, ripples through his torso, shoulders, and throat, reaching his lips as Tom kisses him. Tom's lips are soft, barely touching Jean's, and the anticipation and longing makes Jean tremble again. He strains his neck to kiss Tom fully on the mouth.

On solstice, Tom did not kiss Jean. Jean is surprised at how well their lips fit together; surprised and, also, vindicated. He could kiss Tom forever. Jean's arms are still flung out at either side and this feeling, of being both helpless and held, increases the pleasure of the kiss. Tom's buttocks are warm on Jean's crotch, but the droplets of water that fall from him are cold. The nightingale's song crescendos into trills and, despite the late hour, Jean feels like the world is only just waking up. Tom relaxes his grip and Jean pulls Tom's full weight down on top of him. Tom grips Jean's hip with one hand, the other tangled in his hair, and braces himself against the ground with his foot. They move like this, half wrestling, half kissing; sometimes both sitting upright, their legs interlocked or one of them on the ground, disarmed. They are covered in flecks of dirt and grass, their feet muddy from the river, and Jean thinks about the Roman soldiers who fought here, gripping each other with the same fierceness.

Tom steadies Jean against the ground with his left hand, while his right reaches between Jean's legs. It is this that makes Jean finally surrender. With his free hand Jean brings Tom's forehead to his own. When they are not kissing, they breathe into each other's mouths. Beans and smoke and river. The bank is damp and cool; the sun has dipped below the tree line so that when Jean opens his eyes, he sees Tom as if through a film, flattened.

The nightingale finishes her song. Around them the crickets call, and far off, the high-pitched whine of a machine. Noises amplify and recede as Jean grips Tom's shoulder. He bites it to stop himself from calling out; his body is damp—there is a stone digging into his side and his foot has cramp—but he does not feel any of these things, only a single motion spinning him into the red-streaked sky.

After, Jean falls dutifully onto his back and makes a fist for Tom to fuck, but somehow, when Tom angles toward him, it doesn't feel right. Their bodies, once in sync, are awkward, and Tom pulls back, swearing. The cold rushes in and something flicks in Tom's eyes. Is it this, Jean's fear that Tom isn't happy, or is it because Jean feels guilty about being the first to come, or is it because Tom spoke about men fucking men, but Jean finds himself suggesting they can, if Tom wants, do it for real.

If Tom wants.

The first time they try, the pain is blinding. Jean lifts his legs so Tom can rub spit on him. It feels like something is tearing into Jean; or trying to tear out of him. Like the hardest shit he has ever done. Jean bites his own hand, but Tom presses down harder and he can't help crying out. This is not as easy as he thought it would be.

Wait here, Tom says.

As Jean blinks at the thin sky, anticipation hollows his insides. Was this how the Roman soldiers felt as the white cliffs of Dover appeared, rising larger and larger, filling their vision? Tom returns with the butter, soft and melted from the sun.

Grease fills Jean's nostrils as this time, after two, three attempts, Tom slides into him. It still hurts but not in the same way. The smell is rich, cloying, and sweet, and it makes Jean gag. The smell in the campsite bathroom made Jean gag too. Sweet butter and bitter oil and the particular meaty scent of that Italian man. He could not get rid of it no matter how much he washed. Tom pushes and Jean gasps. How much farther can there be?

The window in the bathroom was open. Pale yellow flakes of paint had collected in the sill, revealing the rotten wood beneath. Jean had focused on that; he tries to focus on part of Tom's shoulder now, where a collection of moles gather. The veins in Tom's neck are blue; his face is red. He does not look like he is enjoying this. Neither did the Italian man. Tom thrusts and Jean cries out, he thrusts again and it touches Jean's stomach. At least the pain takes him away from Provence and brings him back to his body.

There is something underneath the pain too. In his centre, a small hot coal; it is fleeting, but Jean has a sense of the fire. When the Italian man groaned, Jean had felt something not dissimilar, a flicker at the base of his pelvis. Then the rich butter and sweet grass is replaced by a pungent, acrid smell. Battle, again. Men in armour running through a muddy field, drenched in rain and blood and shit, running forward, through the earth that clings to their thighs, against the metal that presses their bodies, toward certain death.

They wash in the stream. Jean is sore. Tom finished not inside him but on his stomach. Jean was covered in cum and leaking shit, and he was grateful Tom did not walk away. Jean cleans his stomach, his anus, his thighs. Above them the final colours fade, and the sky turns a muted, gauzy blue. The first stars appear, and far off, the echo of the moon. Jean is reminded of a twice-exposed photograph, one image layered over another. The new thing held by the memory of before. He tugs absentmindedly at his penis, thinking that it would be nice to come again.

The next day they move their camp from Sweet Willow Wood to a stretch of deserted beach directly on the coast. It is another beautiful day, and the sand is bright hot and burning. They strip off and swim before setting up camp, Jean erecting the tent, Tom, the fire. They move around each other quietly and with ease. Although they are not talking, it is different from yesterday's silence. When they both reach for the canteen, their hands brushing, each pulls away self-consciously.

Last night, when they got back to camp, Tom climbed into his sleeping bag and fell asleep immediately. Jean stayed up worrying, but that fear has dissipated throughout today. There are still times when Tom will leave him—his face turning blank, his eyes sunken and hollow, as if someone has turned off his batteries—but these moments don't last for long, and Jean doesn't need to know where he has gone.

They switch between lounging and swimming. Behind them is a small wood where, Jean shows Tom, a beehive sits precariously in the branches of a horse chestnut. Jean makes Tom come with his mouth; Tom makes Jean with his hand. Tom goes wooding for the fire and they cook mackerel they bought from a roadside truck for dinner. The skin blackens and blisters and when they put the fish between two hunks of bread, oil oozes onto their knees. There is ale and more tomato. They lie on the sand and watch the sun dip below the horizon. Jean wants to know if the sun sets at the same point every day and Tom tells him no, it moves with the Earth. They will be fine, Jean thinks and leans back on his elbows, when they go to China. With Tom there, they won't get lost. And with him; he can bring his tent. He can pick herbs. He says this to Tom—I'll bring a book on Chinese plants—but Tom is lying with his eyes closed.

It is properly dark when Tom wakes with a start. Jean has been watching the moon, trying to work out if she is waxing or waning. Before them, the sea, a denser stretch of darkness. Tom lights a cigarette.

You reckon the others are doing it?

What?

The night vigil.

Jean groups together a cluster of burning logs, exposing their glowing bellies.

Never thought about it, he says.

We should.

All night?

Why not?

Jean is sleepy from the sun and the sand, but he does not want to disappoint Tom. He puts another log on top and blows until the fire catches.

We can try. Might be hard.

I've got something.

Tom shows Jean the brown shrivelled things. He got them from Hugo, who got them from Charles Burrows, who has a whole chemist shop in school, apparently. Jean pops a bottle of ale.

Sure.

Jean has taken mushrooms before, but Tom has not, so it is up to Jean to divide them. They could make tea, but the effects would be weaker and, since they've already eaten, they're at a disadvantage. By the look of these, there are no truffles, just heads.

Oh.

They're good. Just less intense.

Shall we take more?

Tom inspects the small pile in his hand. When Jean took shrooms with Kelly, she alarmingly turned into a life-size doll.

This is fine, he says.

Before, he ate them with a spoonful of honey, but since they have none, they'll have to take them straight. Tom makes a face,

Fuck that's disgusting, downing most of the ale, and Jean is left with water to wash away the bitterness.

What do we do now?

Wait.

How long does it take?

Depends.

Tom's shirt is open, revealing his stomach. His shorts are bunched at his thighs. He is pink all over.

We'll need visas, Jean says.

For what?

China.

Tom grunts and falls onto his back.

You know George can shoot a pheasant from over forty yards.

Cool.

And he's the fastest number six on the team, the rest call him The Engine.

The team?

Rowing. And he can ride.

This is the first time Tom has spoken about George since he died. Tom talks about him in the present tense.

But George hasn't done mushrooms. He never will now.

How do you know?

He hates hippies.

Jean laughs. I'm not a hippie.

You know what I mean.

It's bullshit.

Your praying and shit.

You mean meditation.

I'm probably the first person in my family to ever take drugs, Tom says. Then: Are you feeling anything?

Meditation is not a hippie thing.

I'm thirsty.

Famous people do it.

Exactly.

Everyone in China. They're Communists. Meditation is the opposite of hippie, total opposite.

Above them, the stars spread across the sky. Jean will never get over the stars. In London you rarely see them, more often the sky is clogged with thick smog. They seem especially bright tonight.

Can't imagine Chairman Mao saying *totally groovy my dudes*, Jean says.

There is silence from the other side of the fire. When Jean sits up, Tom is staring at the flames.

Tom?

At first, Jean thinks Tom has sunk into one of his moods. Then the other boy turns, slowly, eyes wide, mouth slack. Is he having a bad reaction? But when Tom sees Jean, his face crumples into joy. Jean feels it too. The creeping sensation all over him. The sand beneath him and on him and the sea within him. The air. The moon. The fire. These things take on a new significance, working in harmony to create this single night just for them. It is so nice. Jean smiles, wide, mimicking Tom's, which grows until they are both grinning, now laughing. Jean does not remember ever feeling this happy. The mushrooms are good.

They walk down to the sea, enjoying the way the sand shifts beneath their feet. They strip where it becomes compact and cool. They swim and the water feels like velvet. Jean tries to explain that meditation is like the water, but he can't remember what Bruce Lee said and anyway, Tom is laughing again, and

Jean is too. They spend some time being shells, curled into balls side by side. Then birds, running up and down the beach, emitting shrill calls, and lastly, fish. Tom believes that in another life he was a bird, but Jean disagrees. Watching the flames illuminate Tom's flushed skin, Jean sees that Tom is a fox.

What are you? Tom asks.

What do you reckon?

Tom regards him, Not sure yet. He puts an arm around Jean's shoulder, curling him inward. Yes, Jean has never been so happy.

The night is long, though, and after they have talked about what animals they would be, and Tom has told Jean more facts about George, and Jean has spouted more facts about China, there seems to be nothing left to say. They deliberate taking more. Jean takes a piss by the bushes behind their tent, and it is here that he sees it.

Look.

What is it?

Guess.

It's not.

I told you: It grows everywhere.

I don't believe you.

Look at it.

Fuck, Tom says. Put it down.

Jean spins the stem between his fingers, the fluffy white blooms blurring, the serrated leaves fanning out. He brushes Tom's nose.

Are you fucking crazy?

Let's take it.

What?

You and me.

Tom looks properly afraid. His voice shakes when he says, You're joking.

Why not?

Jean, come on.

Chicken.

Jean raises the plant to his lips.

Jean.

He puts a bloom in his mouth, crushing the petals with his teeth. Tom's face is pale, knuckles white where his hands are clamped together. As Jean bites another flower, Tom tries to grab the stem.

You fucking maniac! Tom is shouting.

Wait, Jean says, trying to dodge him, but Tom isn't listening, swinging for him.

Jean runs, Tom chasing, all along the beach, around the tents and back to the bushes. Tom has a wild look in his eyes. When Jean trips on a root by the woods, Tom pounces. Jean tries to fight him off, but Tom is sticking his fingers into Jean's mouth. He gets more sand in there than he retrieves weed out. He is still screaming, and is he crying? Finally, Jean manages to wrestle him off and say, between coughs:

Parsley.

Tom is holding a fistful of his own hair. Jean crouches in front of him.

Tom. It's not hemlock. It's wild parsley.

What happens next happens as if in slow motion. Tom hits Jean, square on the jaw, and Jean falls backward, hitting the trunk of the horse chestnut and knocking the beehive above. A few bees fall to the ground, droning quietly. Tom, still tense with fear, panics and bats at them, and the insects, also afraid, retaliate.

Tom's cheek has swollen to an ugly discoloured yellow. Jean's face hurts but he doesn't think about that right now. It took him some time to calm Tom down, and still Tom hasn't really spoken. Jean underestimated the strength of Tom's high, and he is sorry, now, remembering how scared he'd been of Kelly the doll. He sat Tom by the fire with the canteen of water while he made a poultice out of chickweed and mud.

This is going to hurt.

Tom winces as Jean applies the paste to his cheek.

How do you know this shit?

What?

This. Hemlock, that crazy leek thing.

I don't know.

Come on.

It wasn't all princesses and ogres and early morning walks with Rosa. Some things he learned the hard way. In the campsite toilet there had been a bee. As Rosa applied the same poultice to Jean that he now spreads on Tom's cheek, she had asked Jean what he did to make the bee angry. Her hair fell in loose strands around her face and her eyes were dark shadows. When he told her the bee was trapped, she said, Why are you always doing something stupid? Tom makes a noise like a kettle whistling.

Fine, fuck it. I don't care.

I'm sorry.

You never tell me anything.

Tom takes Jean's face in his hands and pulls him close. He must still be high.

Who are you, Blondie?

What Jean didn't tell Rosa, what he can't tell Tom, was that he was trapped too. It was early, before most of the campsite was awake. Jean didn't know how long the Italian man had been standing there, watching him. Had he seen him piss? Backlit in the bathroom door, he seemed stockier. He came toward Jean with the same bounding movements, talking lightly about Jean's shorts. He was touching the fabric, complimenting the colour, asking if he bought them nearby. Jean found himself in a stall, the man pressing against him. From where he stood, Jean could see the man's soft bald spot. He could feel his erection.

What the fuck is wrong with you? Tom says, knocking over the paste. Stop it. Stop looking at me like that.

Jean scoops as much of the paste as he can back into the billy.

I'm talking to myself, Tom says.

There is not much left and what Jean salvages is ruined with dirt and twigs. His hands are covered in grime.

I'm not a fucking mind reader. That first night, I didn't think you would be at the spot, Tom says.

I was.

Yeah, but you never said you would. If you don't tell me, I don't know.

Jean is silent.

Then you do some psycho shit like try to kill yourself.

It was parsley.

It wasn't funny, Tom says and his voice cracks.

For two years, two *years*, Tom says, I've wondered what goes on inside that head.

And something opens inside Jean. Does this mean Tom has been aware of Jean as long as Jean has been of him? He is surprised. He thought he had shown Tom how much he wants to be here; he thought it was obvious, seeping out of him like sweat. But now Tom is telling him that he wants more, has wanted more for a long time. Jean tries not to think about the wasted paste. Instead, he focuses on the fact that Tom is here, cracking him open like an egg.

I don't know who the fuck you are.

Jean could tell Tom that there is no other option, will never be any other option for him, but he does not have the words for this. The paste on the ground has dried, forming a thin, pale coating. Jean could tell Tom about Rosa, but he senses that this will not satisfy him. Tom is asking Jean to give him something he has not given anyone else. All weekend he has been probing, as if he knows there is something going on at the back of Jean's mind. As if he already knows about the Italian man. Jean feels the confession being pulled from him like a piece of string.

I got stung in France, he says. There was a man.

The sea crashes behind them; it seems both closer and farther away. Jean's lower back aches, his jaw is throbbing. The mushrooms drain from him. He pours the last of the paste onto the ground. He is embarrassed, remembering how the Italian man flirted with him, asking him what he liked, if he'd ever been fucked properly, and, in response to Jean's startled, furtive, No, taking Jean's hand and placing it deep in his flies. The heat of the night before, the thick hardness. Tom is quiet, watching him.

Yeah, there was this man.

He does not tell Tom much: not that the man told him to spit, told him to rub it, to put it in his mouth. The open window, the flecks of paint. The bee. But in the silence that follows, Jean knows that Tom understands. Tom is staring at him. He moves his leg away from Jean and Jean turns, chucking the billy to one side.

Stupid. This is not what Tom meant when he said he wanted to know Jean. Of course it isn't. Jean feels sick, imagining what Tom must be thinking. The worst part is that the man did not threaten Jean. Rather, he spoke in a way that was so self-assured, so certain, as if he knew what Jean was and what he wanted to do. If the man had pushed it, Jean might have let him fuck him. It was only when Jean was on his knees that things got a bit rough. And it was only much later Jean realised he'd been stung.

Tom coughs, rubs a hand over his face.

It's fine, Jean says, and builds up the fire.

The air has the thin quality of predawn. It is cold. Jean focuses on laying branch on branch. He doesn't want to look at Tom because of what he might see there. In Tom's mind, Jean asked for it. He deserved it. But then Tom touches his arm, steadying his hand. It is brief and fleeting, but it is what Jean needs.

I hate George, Tom says quietly.

The sky gathers pace around them, Jean's teeth chatter.

No, you don't.

You're right. Hated.

Come on.

I'm always going on about how great he is. Truth is, I was scared of him.

Jean wraps his arms around his knees and rests his chin. He knows that Tom is trying to make him feel better, and he does.

Once, he locked me in a suitcase. Left me there for three hours. I pissed myself.

Jean scoffs.

Any beer left?

Tom rolls a cigarette, and they share the last ale. The first gulls fly overhead, calling. Jean has that empty feeling he gets after vomiting. They climb into their sleeping bags and huddle in the opening of the tent.

I don't want to go back, Tom says.

Me neither.

Three days after the funeral, my pa has me in his office, says I'm to learn the ropes after exams.

Jean lets this new information settle.

Straight after? He tries to keep his voice neutral.

Yeah, Tom says. Fucking pain in the arse.

Tom reaches for the ale and, before taking it, brushes Jean's face.

That shouldn't look so bad in the morning.

Does Tom realise that if he is going home straight after exams, he won't be able to come to China? Jean wants to ask but something holds him back. He has said too much already. They both have. Were Tom's silences throughout the day about George, or were they, in fact, about something else? Has Tom been waiting to break the news to him? Jean recalls how Tom avoided talking about China every time Jean brought it up. Worse, did Tom never expect that they would go? Jean knows this is what Tom thinks because a part of him, too, didn't believe it would ever happen.

After, the Italian man patted Jean on the head and tugged his erection. Jean didn't feel truly bad until that evening, when, upon entering the restaurant, he saw Rosa and the man sitting together on the high seats at the bar, her head thrown back in laughter.

We did it, Tom says. Look.

It is true, the sky is bright. Is this what David meant when he told them to do a night vigil? At least Jean can return saying I am changed.

They will walk in different directions so they return to school separately. Jean wanted to walk part of the way together, but Tom was insistent, and Jean cannot help but feel that Tom is sick of him. Does Tom realise that this is it: there will be exams and, after, it will be over. The past two days have felt like their own little universe. There was a part of Jean that thought it would never end, but reality, as sure as light, has seeped through. His throat is thick. As Jean turns to go, Tom grabs his arm. Jean sees several things form on his lips: Tom will come to China, Tom isn't gay, Tom loves him. But Tom says:

A swan. That's what you are, Blondie.

Jean recalls the fox he saw on his first day, fur stained red around its mouth, and a few metres farther, the battlefield, white feathers sprayed across the ground, spiralling toward the bloodied body. It is rare, but when desperate, foxes hunt swans.

X

IT IS THE DAY AFTER THE WILDERNESS TRIP. THE BILLIARD table has been covered with a sheet of wood, transforming it into a desk around which Hugo, Tom, Percy, Theo, Colin, and Jean sit. Samuel lies on the sofa. They are meant to be studying for their upcoming O-level exams but instead they are talking about Charles Burrows, who has disappeared. No warning, no goodbye, no final lesson.

He killed someone, Theo says.

Where's the body? says Colin.

This p-place, Percy stammers, Is an op-pen grave.

Who'd he kill, Sherlock?

Townie.

Some p-poor bitch.

Brought her back.

Just as she's about to take her clothes off— Samuel chimes in.

He grabs her by the throat!

Theo and Samuel dive on Colin, who fights them off and scampers across the room.

It is another boiling day, and the room is stuffy. Outside, the grass is pale and brittle from a lack of rain and the shouts of boys in the distance reach them muffled. Theo and Samuel edge toward Colin, but when he flicks open his knife, they back away, resuming their former positions: Theo chain smoking at the table, Samuel sprawled across the sofa. Hugo, who has been surprisingly silent, throws a ball methodically against the wall, grubbing the red-flocked paper with each hit.

Jean doodles in his painfully empty exercise book. It is too hot to study, and he also can't stop thinking about the unexpected absence of their teacher. Jean got back late last night, after managing to twist his ankle in the final mile. The rest of them had stayed up but only because David made them. When Jean hobbled in, Tom said, Finally, fuck's sake, before they streamed out. It was only when they were alone that David broke the news to Jean: There were no more lessons, in the morning they would start studying for exams, and Charles Burrows had left the school. Jean wanted to know why, but David said, in an uncharacteristically stern tone, For God's sake Jean, none of your bullshit right now. Then, quieter, regretfully, Let's just get through these final two weeks, OK?

As Jean slumps across the table, the doodle before him growing into a karate master attacking a group of schoolgirls, he, too, wants to know what happened to Charles. What, exactly, Charles did. Theo stubs a cigarette in a gilt ashtray and lights a new one.

Let's be honest, he says. Charlie wouldn't kill a girl.

Hugo, without pausing from throwing the ball says, You're a fucking moron.

Theo holds up his hands in mock apology. Someone got up on the wrong side.

You want to go? Hugo stands. I'll break your fucking face.

Jesus, Hugo.

Samuel looks nervously at the two of them. There is something unreadable there. Hugo's face is gaunt and morose and flushed with emotion.

Maybe he didn't kill someone, Samuel says. Maybe he was a leader, you know, in one of those cults.

Like Charles M-Manson, Percy says and perks up, and Theo runs with it: He's always been a bit of a weirdo. What was that thing he used to wear? With the bells? I wouldn't be surprised.

Hugo snorts, leans back.

Charles Burrows has always been unconventional, pushing the limitations of what is acceptable, but it is only now that he has gone, Jean considers the significance of his quirks. Lying on the floorboards in a darkened classroom, listening to *Under Milk Wood*. Stamping through the hall, banging pots and pans, and reciting Tennyson like an odd marching band. More recently, his teaching had become erratic: like after solstice when he passed out, or in what, Jean realises now, was their last class together, when he was manic.

The boys had arrived to find Charles billowing around the room in a tatty velvet robe. The sleeves were adorned with bells and each time he raised his arms, which was often, they would be showered with a cacophony of sound. He was unshaved, his moustache uncharacteristically bushy, his hair uncombed. As he ushered them in on a wave of tinkling motions, arranging them on the floor around a Japanese tea ceremony, Jean noticed the dark circles under his eyes and the yellow tinge to his complexion. It is a special occasion, Charles trilled, prancing between the boys and tapping them lightly on the head, as if he were playing Duck, Duck, Goose. Sometimes he prattled quickly, other times, he lost track midsentence. He was jerky and unstable, kneeling on the floor to pour the tea. When Percy asked him what they were celebrating, Charles swung round to face him—What was that?—pot still angled, so that a steaming arc cut across Jean's lap. Jean cried out, but Charles did not notice, continuing to douse the carpet in the woody, hot tea, and blinking somewhere above their heads.

My mum says it was the state, Theo says now, returning to Charles Manson. After '68 the government was shitting themselves, weren't they? Needed to get control of things again.

You saying that the US government killed thirty people? Colin is carving into the wooden board across the table.

Thirty-five.

I'm saying it was in their interest.

Fuck hippies.

Exactly. Fuck hippies.

After the tea episode, the rest of the lesson was chaotic. They were meant to be studying *Hamlet*, but when Hugo read for Gertrude, Charles interrupted him, squeezing his cheeks and telling him to *feel* the lines. Hugo stared at his book and the others could feel his embarrassment. At one point, Charles stood on the table and told them all to howl, howl like Hamlet would have done. The boys remained silent, avoiding each other's eyes. Abruptly, Charles gave up; bored or disappointed, he slouched in the armchair, muttering to himself, a fat and unkempt Plato in his lap.

Jean cannot remember who asked if they could go, but he does remember the way Charles said, staring at them with bloodshot eyes, Fuck off. Just fuck off.

It was only when he was halfway across the field that Jean remembered his bag with his cough drops tin, left behind. When Jean returned, Charles was asleep. There were two deep lines in his forehead, and Jean thought he looked much older than twenty-six. As Jean watched him, Plato lifted her trembling bottom and released a torrent of dark brown pellets, some falling to the floor, others sticking, hot and stinking, in Charles's lap.

What's going to happen to Plato and Socrates? Jean asks now.

I heard Angora is delicious, Theo says.

Savages, Samuel says.

How about Manson's tattoo, Hugo says. He seems jittery when the subject strays to their teacher. He looks at Jean as he says, Great little tattoo Manson had on his forehead, wasn't it?

He did the *x* during the trial, Percy says, quietly. Like a t-target.

It's not an *x* though is it, Hugo says, still looking at Jean. Jean feels, rather than sees, the boys' eyes shift over him.

It wasn't a swasti-sti-ka originally, Percy continues. It's a pp-political st-st-st-statement.

Hugo stammers incomprehensibly at Percy, and the other boy blinks at the table.

Jean could forgive Charles Burrows the drinking, forgive him the outbursts of anger and the falling asleep, but there had been something so rank about the rabbit shitting on him that he could not excuse it. It was not just the animal's excrement, hotly stinking up the room, but Charles's total lack of awareness, that made Jean's stomach turn and cast Charles in a new light. Instead of eccentric teacher, he was a fucking mess. Was that what got him fired? Did David clue up to Charles's wayward ways and cast him out? Or was there another reason? Some specific, terrible transgression that David could not ignore. On the horizon dark clouds gather and the air is saturated. Sweat trickles down his neck.

As if following the same train of thought Theo says, Maybe Charlie nicked something.

Look at this, Hugo gestures toward a painting. How much you reckon it's worth?

Mate, this is a missed opportunity, Colin says, perking up. Look at how much shit is here. We could make a killing.

Using the crutch David gave him, Jean swings himself over to the window seat and stretches his leg along the faded cushion. Nurse bandaged his ankle last night but it still throbs. He leans his head out of the window. He can see the younger boys running in the distance, points of static against the sky. Behind him they argue about whether Colin could sell loot from the school; Colin is adamant his dad knows someone on Portobello Market, and Hugo is interested. The only problem is transportation. But Colin is sure he can borrow his dad's van. Tom, who has been silent throughout, is bent over his exercise book, although Jean can see he is not writing. On their last morning, Tom had zipped together their sleeping bags so for the few hours they slept, his hot, naked body curved against Jean's. Jean liked the feeling of Tom's soft penis against his buttocks more than fucking.

For fuck's sake, Tom says now, angry. We all know why he's gone.

The others falter and something clicks into place for Jean.

Hugo has gone a sickly green and is staring at Tom, threatening but also—is it?—pleading. Jean recalls the former French teacher and student: the torrid love affair that no one suspected, the barricade they set up in one of the wings with the banner, "Vive La Révolution," the scandal when the local papers got hold of the story, the rumour that David bribed them not to print it. Imagine the outcry if something similar happened again. "Troubled Boys' School Front for Gay Sex Trafficking." That would decimate admissions, even if Compton Manor is a last resort for most.

David would not want to risk another disgrace. If he were to find a teacher involved with a boy—and now Jean recalls Hugo coming out of Charles's rooms, flushed; Charles pouring Hugo a drink; Charles's fingers lingering on top of Hugo's head—he would deal with it swiftly and cleanly. Better not to get the boys' parents involved (especially not those parents who sit on the board, who donate a large sum, yearly), better to keep the whole thing hushed. Jean is surprised Charles chose Hugo and not him; then again, perhaps it was not Charles who chose, perhaps it was Hugo who pounced. The boys are silent, waiting for Tom to expound. He seems about to, but then Theo cuts in:

Yeah, yeah, we know. Charles was the biggest fuck up between here and Dover. But do you have to ruin all our fun by being so serious all the time, Peterson? Can't you allow us our little fantasies?

Tom grumbles something about being a good sport when it matters, and the tension drains from the room. Hugo chucks the ball at Samuel. Samuel turns for cover, but the ball hits him square in the groin. Hugo follows through by slapping him on the head. Is this really the boy Charles was fucking? Perhaps the reason Charles is gone is the simplest: As Theo says, Charles was a drunk.

Anyway, it doesn't matter, Tom says. The point is, he's fucked us. Months of listening to his bullshit. What are we meant to write on the exam?

Samuel climbs over the back of the sofa and slumps on the floor. Since when do you care?

I don't. Tom flicks a rubber at him.

Do any of us? Hugo says. I mean, does anyone even need these bloody exams?

Colin, who has been walking around the room, inspecting the contents, says, The trick is to take only a few bits from each room.

Start with a painting, Theo says.

The conversation slides into what artwork would be most valuable, but what Hugo said, about not needing to take the exams, niggles at Jean. For Jean, the exams are like the rainclouds, threatening and inevitable and necessary.

Colin suggests paintings of the armoured figures, but Theo dismisses these as too unwieldy. He prefers the paintings of fruit—fruit, which his mother says is timeless. It is Hugo who tells them that it doesn't matter what is painted but rather by whom. Hugo stands with Colin and points to a small oil of a pear.

See the quality of the paint here? The way it's thick. And the little dots. This could be really old. This could be worth something.

Shit.

What are we waiting for?

The surprise Jean first felt turns to sickly unease. How does Hugo know this stuff? He finds himself asking the question aloud. Hugo snorts, and Colin looks at him in disbelief.

You know who his dad is, right?

The name rings a tiny bell in Jean's mind, but he still needs Theo to explain. Which he does, incredulously, Hugo interjecting that he told them the Yid was a retard. As it turns out, Hugo's father is only the most famous living British artist. This comes to Jean like a blow. Who would have thought: Hugo, the child of rich bohemians, growing up on the estate in Cornwall, visiting the townhouse in London, and going to Ruskin Art School where his father has made a sizeable donation. Jean understands, now, why Hugo doesn't care about exams: his place at art school is guaranteed.

Ruskin is where Rosa wants Jean to go. The sculpture department is, apparently, unparalleled, and he could develop his ceramics.

When Jean was little, she would set him up in her studio, his chubby fingers pressing into the soft clay. The feel of it so pleasant and cool. He spent a lot of time between the ages of ten and fourteen crafting bobbling shapes from the brown stuff. Looking at Giacometti and trying to copy those primal figures. He even learned how to throw. Those were good times with Rosa in a period that was frequently disrupted by tremendous rows. He liked going to Camberwell (where she taught) and spending hours in the ceramics studio, the magic of the kiln, his pots and cups and whatever else emerging new and glossy and hard. Rosa was gently encouraging, making him feel like he was doing something worthwhile.

But then Rosa took him to visit Ruskin along with twelve of her students. Staring up at the scenes of medieval scholars carved out of stone, Jean, who was already an outsider in the group of chatty, hippie students, felt even more out of place. Rosa held his hand and he could feel the hushed caution of the students behind him, speculating on why Jean, who at fifteen was only a few years younger than them, was being treated like a five-year-old.

Jean was determined not to satisfy their curiosity, but his frustration mounted as, in each room they passed through Rosa spoke in an ever-increasing stage whisper—Isn't that *nice* Jean, Wouldn't you *like* that?—so that, when they reached the kilns, and the final part of the tour, when Rosa encouraged him to stand at the front, Jean had had enough. He shrugged her off and, in the process, knocked over a table of display ceramics. It may not have been so bad had Rosa not made such a big deal of it, saying, even though Jean was there, He doesn't mean it, he can't *help* it.

Jean's love of ceramics was destroyed that day. Jean liked them precisely because they weren't school: Why would he want to ruin that by studying them? When he came to Compton Manor, he did not use the pottery studio, which was probably why he did not know that Hugo did.

Theo is going to America to work for his grandfather's hedge fund. Theo, who talks loudly about women's arseholes and tits, who himself is not impartial to dressing up in their clothes, who screams like a pagan when jumping over a fire; Theo, whose WASP mother is a raging (if rich) hippie, the disgrace of her family; whose Jamaican father is a cabbie; this Theo is going to become, of all things, a banker.

Percy speaks Greek because his mother is from Athens; his English father left them when he was little: he is going to do an advanced course in business management before joining her to help run their hotel empire. He is also not stressed about exams. Partly because he is the smartest boy in the school, partly because, like Hugo and the rest, he has something waiting for him when he leaves.

Samuel will work in the office of his father's construction company and Colin—Colin, who is forever carving stupid patterns—is becoming a carpenter.

Their conversation layers over Jean, giving him the repeated sensation of whiplash. Tom is right, it doesn't matter why Charles disappeared; once again, Jean has been focusing on the wrong thing. He has emerged, blinking and awake, to find that everyone has been getting on. When did these boys start thinking about their futures?

I've always wanted to be a carpenter, Colin says.

Hugo is saying he will go to America with Theo before art school to do some travelling, and Percy might join them, Colin too, and even Samuel is invited.

What about you, Peterson?

I've got the farm, Tom says.

Just for the summer.

Come on, Peterson!

Jean avoids looking at Tom, whose answer is noncommittal, but which is also not a no, aware that so recently Tom told him he could not go to China.

Later, when Jean is smoking by the pit of the new swimming pool, Tom finds him.

You know, Tom says, In ancient Rome there were these virgin priestesses. He fingers the joint. They had to keep this fire lit day and night.

Jean takes a hard drag.

The flame was sacred. And if it went out, guess what?

Jean blows the smoke through his nostrils. He doesn't look at Tom when Tom grips his shoulder and says, They buried them alive.

Tom has not spoken to Jean since they returned from the hike. In fact, he has been in a worse mood, picking on Jean intermittently. When Samuel, who did not go on the trip on account of his asthma, asked the boys how it was, Tom described his twenty-seven-mile hike and camping on the beach. He said he'd been chased by boys in Bexhill and made a paste for the bruises. Hence the discoloration on his face. When Samuel asked what he used, he said dandelion, which was wrong, but Jean did not correct him. The other boys admired his ingenuity.

When it was Jean's turn, he didn't know what to say, their final morning flickering in his mind. How he had turned to face Tom in the sleeping bag, the other boy nuzzling closer, counting the freckles on his face. Tom had laughed harshly, announcing to the room, Jean got lost. Jean thought Tom was afraid he would say something. But when the other boys detailed their trips—Theo did the night vigil and Percy, too, without a fire; Colin caught, skinned, and cooked his own rabbit; he took only a tarpaulin and made his own pegs from wood; Theo walked to a lake farther south and fished for his supper—Jean suspected Tom was angry simply because Jean had been there. Slowing him down. Stopping him from, what? An authentic experience? Hugo fucked off the hike and visited his girlfriend in Hastings.

Now, Jean wonders why Tom has come up to him. Why he is talking about virgins. And he realises, he doesn't care.

Fuck you, Jean says.

Tom stares at him, hard, like he is about to hit him. Jean has often wondered what Tom sees when he looks at him. He seems, at times, not to see Jean at all. Jean's leg is propped up awkwardly next to him. He wouldn't be much good in a fight. Tom sighs, squints at the sun.

Do you ever try, Tom says, stamping a clump of dirt into the pit, I don't know, try helping yourself?

The question is so stupid Jean does not answer it.

I know it's stressful, Tom says. I'm stressed.

More dirt kicked into the pit, the joint passed back.

Look, Tom says, Charlie gave Hugo some speed before he left.

Tom's hands are firm and warm on Jean's shoulders. His breath smells like weed and mints. His freckles are dark against his pink skin.

It's meant to help.

The conversation lingers in Jean's mind as he limps back to school. Jean wishes his ankle was better; he's barely reached the terrace, despite the crutch. He is unsettled. Not just by the fact that Charles has disappeared, or that the boys have plans when they finish school, or that Tom is serious about studying, but because there are things about these boys that are not so different from him. Things about which he is ashamed—like Hugo's father is an artist, like Percy's is not around. Things he considered made him stand apart, but which he has discovered are shared. Perhaps he could have been friends with them. He could have spoken about his father or Rosa. He could have been less distant, been more friendly. What was it Tom said, try to help yourself? It is too late now.

By the time he gets to the rabbit hutch, he is sweating. The hutch is dark and still. Charles running across the lawn, red streaming down his arms, the rabbit choking on its own blood. A cave in the earth, opening to the stench of human remains. The alcohol on David's breath last night. He covers his mouth and braces himself, but when he can see again, there is nothing there. And he wishes, with a ferocity that turns his stomach, that he had woken Charles up and told him he was covered in shit. He wishes he had brushed Plato's fur until it was smooth.

XI

IT IS NOW A WEEK SINCE CHARLES BURROWS DISAPPEARED, Jean's ankle has healed, and he has written an essay on almost all the main characters in *Hamlet*. Gertrude is his last one. Tom says he will lend Jean his biology and history notes and, honestly, Jean gave up on maths a long time ago. No amount of speed will fix that. Still, it helps. Before, Jean's mind was like a radio caught between two stations, but now it tunes into one. He has never been able to sit for so long or to write so much. Jean braces himself to tackle the Gertrude essay question, but then David pops his head around the door.

Don't work yourself to the bone.

Just another hour, Davey, Tom says.

Only Tom and Jean are taking speed because Hugo, despite being the provider of the drug, doesn't need to take it; he doesn't need exams. Theo, Percy, Colin, and Samuel don't know about it. Tom says he can't trust them. We could get kicked out for this shit, Tom told Jean on the second night, when they were in the toilet, Tom lifting the key deftly to his own nose, more gingerly toward Jean's. Jean said he would be careful, and Tom told him not to speak, he was going to blow the speed away.

Tom continues to prattle about how he's feeling good about exams, especially history, which is no surprise given their excellent teacher.

A good teacher is only the sum of his students, David smirks.

Jean takes a long drink of water to avoid looking at David and to give his hands something to do. At the back of his throat, the water mixes with the vestiges of the drug, creating a sour, metallic taste that makes him gag. He glugs the water, drinking more to get rid of the bitter taste, downing it because now that he has started, he can't stop.

Tom is still talking to David, telling him that the study club is going well. Jean finishes the water with a gasp and then, embarrassingly, a burp. A long, guttural sound like something small has died inside him. David frowns and Jean studies the table, hiding his dilated pupils. He is not paying attention, therefore, when he sets the glass down, which is why he places it precariously on the edge, only realising his mistake when he lifts his hand away and the glass falls.

The noise is disproportionately loud in the quiet room, and the three of them look at where the glass lies shattered. The shards are strangely beautiful in the dim lamp light, and Jean is tempted to say that—doesn't it look beautiful?—but then David smacks the table.

What did you do that for?

Despite having worked all week, Jean has been twitchy.

Underneath his focus is the rushing exhilaration of the drug, the sense that something is about to happen. The first time he took speed he made the mistake of sitting next to Samuel, who had a small rubber man and that was Jean's whole afternoon gone. It didn't matter that the other boys noticed; that Samuel asked him if he was OK, and that Hugo said the retard had finally lost it. Jean stayed twinging those little rubber arms until Tom dragged him from the room. There are two elements, then, to taking speed: 1) the acute focus, and 2) the desire to *do* something. Jean could feel it rising in him as David and Tom talked, his impatience, waiting for David to leave.

So, although Jean did not consciously drop the glass, as he says to David, It was an accident, there is a small part of him that wonders if he did, in fact, mean to.

David seems to sense this and stands there staring at him. But Tom is on his feet and clearing it up, and David says, Just get rid of it.

At the lake, they cut into the woods. The path is hidden but they know it well. Jean could follow it in his sleep: through the bushes, around the thorns, careful of the tree root, under that low-hanging branch, and into the clearing, like stepping into a spotlight.

What's up? Tom says, hand on Jean's crotch.

The good thing about speed is that you don't need to eat or sleep. The bad thing is that your dick goes limp. Jean can't sit still. He unlaces his shoes and stands by the lake's edge, watching the way the moonlight shreds the water. He dips his toe, and the cold shivers through him. Of course, earlier wasn't the first time Jean smashed something on purpose. When he was eight, he broke all the glass in the house. Jean does not remember why but he remembers methodically collecting water glasses, vases, candlesticks, and smashing them in Rosa's studio.

Jean.

The sharpness in Tom's voice brings Jean back to the clearing, the grass, Tom lying there, face open like the moon.

Come here.

But Jean lingers by the water, watching the ripples on the lake's surface. He had started in the kitchen, when he was eight, taking the green bowls Rosa used for special occasions and the large platter she used for cakes. Next, the living room, where Rosa had a collection of fine figurines, candlesticks, and a vase. There was the bathroom with the series of bottles Rosa had picked up from France. And her studio with its endless jam jars filled with paint brushes and sticks of charcoal. Her perfume, a squat thing that smelled like lemon and sunshine. Each of these objects he gathered, lining them up in her studio.

At first, Rosa thought he was playing a game, but, really, it was about efficiency. So that when he started smashing, which he did, first with one of the figurines, its slender neck splintering, he could continue without pausing. Rosa asked him what the hell he was doing, but quickly fell silent. That's something else he remembers: the silence in the room so that, as he brought down each item, the noise of the glass, sometimes like bells, other times like a high-pitched shriek, rang out. It was like that earlier, in the classroom. The sound of the glass harsh and brittle in the quiet room. And now, the silence of this night, Tom lying behind him expectantly. Jean throws a rock, and it lands with a heavy splosh in the water. Somewhere, an owl calls, breathy, hollow. Jean knows he should turn to Tom, but he can't, not yet.

Next, he smashed the larger objects: a jelly bowl shaped like a bunch of grapes and a blue-patterned vase. The bookends that clanged against the floorboards and took three blows before they finally broke. Some things were too solid—ramekins, for example. Others popped like bubbles—champagne flutes. By the time Jean was breaking these, there was no longer silence in the room, rather, the sound of his own sobbing. Once everything was broken, he surveyed the space, covered in pieces of broken glass. He realised, then, that Rosa had left him, and he wondered how long he had been alone. He crouched on the floor, pressing his knees to his chest, the exhilaration seeping out of him like water down a drain. It was in this position that Dinah found him. Yes, it was Dinah, Rosa's student, friend, colleague, family, who came. Who opened the door with a bucket and a mop and said, voice cheerful as if nothing was wrong, Shall we clear this up then?

Jean.

Tom's voice is quieter, plaintive even. Jean is turned away. Dinah had wrapped him in her arms and run him a bath, saying over and over, It's OK, it's all OK. But Jean could tell she was afraid.

Jean.

Tom is behind Jean now, pressing his body against Jean's back, radiating warmth. Jean winds his fingers in Tom's. Tom rests his chin on Jean's collarbone.

I didn't finish my essay, Jean says. About Gertrude.

Shit, Tom says.

I know.

You *are* taking this seriously, Blondie.

Reckon she'll be on the exam?

Fuck knows.

Tom kisses Jean's neck softly, lightly, and Jean shivers. Jean has believed for a long time that there is something wrong with him. Certainly, when the glass broke in the classroom, he felt the thrill of doing it when he was eight, the memory of that time rushing in, and he was tempted to take Tom's glass and smash it too. And when David said, What did you do that for? Jean felt the familiar feeling of shame rise in him. But also, something else, like anger but sharper.

The strange thing was, when Jean was eight, no one asked him why he did it; not Dinah at the time, nor Rosa, later. In fact, she behaved as if nothing had happened and the episode with the glass has remained, unspoken but remembered, like a spectre between them, evidence to Jean that he is, in some way, broken. But David's question in the classroom dislodged something. As if Jean was waiting to be asked. Yes, he is sure, now, as he stands by the lake with Tom, that there *was* a reason when he was eight. Just as there had been no reason—it was an accident—in the classroom. When he was eight, he did it because of something, or someone. But who? An image hovers at Jean's consciousness now, shadowy, its contours unclear. As Jean presses into Tom's back, he feels it clearing, becoming substantial, but then Tom nips him on the ear, an owl calls, and it evaporates.

Let's go camping, Jean says.

Jean, Tom sighs.

A couple weeks.

Tom groans.

Two weeks.

Jean.

Three, tops.

Tom turns Jean around and kisses him, holding him firmly. He bites Jean's lip, working his way down his neck and along his collarbone. He kisses Jean's side, his stomach, his belly button, the inside of his thigh. His mouth is on Jean and this time Jean is hard. The grass is flattened and soft beneath them. The owl calls again, and above them, the stars, like someone has injected the sky with liquid gold.

But after, the dread returns. Why did he break all the glass? As they walk back to school, this question lingers, accentuated by the flickering static of speed and the rising dawn. Jean's jaw and lower back ache, his mouth tastes nasty and there is a pressure behind his eyes. After they had both come, Jean brought up a camping trip again, but Tom was noncommittal, untangling himself from Jean's grip and saying they should get going.

There is something sickly about the morning sky, the pale lilac beginning to lift. He is sure Tom can feel it, or is it just that he doesn't want to be caught with Jean at four in the morning? Is that why, then, the figure of Hugo seems not simply menacing but fatal when they come upon him in the billiard room? He is sitting in a dark corner so that when he speaks, it is as if a disembodied voice looms out at them from the gloom.

About time.

Fuck, Tom says.

When Hugo steps into the light, his face is drawn, his cheeks red and enflamed as if he has been crying.

Here, Tom chucks Jean's cough drops tin. Hugo doesn't even try to catch it, and the tin clatters on the desk.

I need to talk to you, Hugo says.

Can it wait?

Hugo shifts his gaze to Jean, a thin, sarcastic smirk curling his mouth. Tell me, Yid, what have you been up to at this hour?

Mate, Tom says.

I hope you've not been a naughty boy.

Shut up.

Charlie was a naughty boy.

Tom grabs the back of Hugo's neck and places a hand over his mouth. Hugo bites him, and Tom swears, still whispering, their voices and actions muted, so that Jean feels like he is watching television with the sound turned down.

Tom grips Hugo's face, and Hugo makes a strangled noise, like that of a kitten.

That bitch. That bitch.

Shit. When?

She just told me.

At first, Jean assumed the *bitch* Hugo referred to was him, but the realisation dawns on him, as Tom says, Will she take care of it? that the bitch is not Jean but a girl somewhere in Hastings. Tom absentmindedly plays with the cough drops tin that lies open on the table, while Hugo explains that she called him earlier tonight, called the school no less. He had to pretend to David that she was a cousin. She was crying, Hugo says. Fucking bitch.

Only days ago, this was the girl Hugo bragged about, sitting on the same table by which he now stands. He said she was the fittest bird in East Sussex, looked just like Lynda Carter in *Wonder Woman*. Acted like her too. Her stamina, apparently, was something even he couldn't compete with; she was begging him for more even when he'd come three times. Hugo's legs had swung in the space below the table, like a schoolboy's. This, combined with the braggadocian nature of his claims, made Jean suspicious. Now, he is impressed that Hugo managed to get a girl to sleep with him.

Jean relaxes, slightly, stepping farther into the room. Despite the drama, this is good news. Hugo does not know about Jean and Tom. The panic that has plagued Jean for hours shifts to euphoria, and a new wave of speed-induced confidence surges through him. Maybe Tom and he will go camping, maybe they will catch the ferry across the sea, burn peat and learn fishing songs.

Hugo takes a sharp inhale, a long exhale, before breaking into dull, repressed sobs. Mate, Tom says, and grips his shoulder, his thumb making small circular motions on Hugo's collarbone.

Maybe, after that, Tom and Jean will move somewhere. Or Tom will want him to come to the farm. He could do that, live in a little cottage on Tom's land, Tom arriving late at night, covered in dirt.

Tom holds Hugo, and the weight of the other boy leans into him. Jean feels benevolent. He is ready to, if not exactly comfort Hugo, commiserate with him.

But then, from between his fingers Hugo says: She says I have to pay, and I've already burned through my allowance.

And Tom says, How could you be so fucking stupid?

At the same time, Jean pulls up a chair, and the noise of metal legs against wooden floor scrapes through the conversation. Hugo sees Jean then; sees Jean witnessing his embarrassment, Tom's anger.

You know he's only fucking you for practice.

Jean may not know why he smashed all the glass when he was eight years old, but he certainly knows why he lunges across the table at Hugo. As he reaches for the other boy, something stops him, and he is surprised to find Tom pushing him backward. Jean is confused. Didn't Tom hear what Hugo just said, isn't this his worst nightmare? He can hear his heartbeat in his ears and his arms are tense. Tom should be helping not hindering him. Tom should be kicking the shit out of Hugo.

That's right, walk away, Hugo says.

Tom turns to Hugo: Mate. You can see he's on edge.

The first rays of sunlight pierce the room, cutting a line across the bookcase, the table, Hugo's body. The school is hushed, but outside the birds sing ferociously. Something in the way Tom spoke gives Jean the sense, once again, that he does not really know what is going on. Tom has always insisted that, after their time together, Jean and he return to school separately. During lessons they do not talk; rarely will Tom even look at Jean. He is rude, if anything, in public.

All this because, Jean thought, Tom wanted to keep what they had safe. How, then, could Hugo know? Has he followed them? A cloud shifts and the beam of light widens, spreading across the room like spilled paint, illuminating the twisting grain of wood, Hugo's face. In the light it cracks open, fragile, and Jean is reminded of how Tom held it between his hands. Their noses pressed together, Hugo's head on Tom's shoulder, Tom's hand on his collarbone. The realisation falls through Jean like a stone. Hugo knows because Tom told him.

At the top of the room, the delicate cornicing blends into an elaborate pattern of fruit, flowers, and small creatures. There is a hunting scene, knights chasing a hare, painted in a fresco on the ceiling. The paint is pale with time but flecks of gold glint on the armour and in the animal's eyes. The beauty of this place still startles Jean, the luxury of it. Every day, he walks into class, or through the grand hall, or even does a shit in the yellow-tiled bathroom, and he is struck by how extravagant it is.

Not Tom and Hugo though. Tom and Hugo, who grew up with houses just as grand, for whom this school is an extension of home. Of course, Jean thinks as his gaze trails down the damask wallpaper, the gilt mantelpiece clock, the velvet chaise, of course Tom told Hugo. He imagines them stretched out on the green leather armchairs of the smoking room, sipping a good scotch and recounting their escapades. Or perhaps they were in the art room, or even the chapel, sniggering like schoolgirls. Just as there is no difference between Compton Manor and home, there is no difference between their lives. They share everything: who they fuck, who they knock up, ready to help when needed—I'll talk to my pa, Tom says stiffly now.

Or perhaps it wasn't said explicitly, something unspoken moving between them. Hugo did not need to be told, knowing Tom as he has for so many years. Jean toes the oriental silk rug with his boot. What lives they have lived together: the bows and arrows, the tree houses, the horse riding, and football, and fishing, and driving. The evenings splayed on plush carpets drinking a vintage nicked from the cellar. A closeness that comes from years of watching each other grow in fits and starts, then leaps. The cut fingers, bruised heads, first kisses, first heartbreaks. Knowing someone so well that you do not need to be told when he is fucking another boy in the school.

Thanks, Hugo says stiffly.

Perhaps Tom did not need to tell Hugo because Jean is not his first. What were Hugo's exact words? Fucking you for practice. Jean thought that when Tom found him on solstice, it was Tom who, like Jean fled Sandra, left Millie. But is the real reason Tom sought out Jean simply that he was horny? When the girls were sent home early for drinking, Tom turned to the next best thing.

The rug is worn in patches and the coarse fibres of its backing appear underneath. Jean scrapes at these, fraying them. What about other boys? What can you get if you go to the back toilets, what happens at the Tuscan arches? Jean has never looked for it because he has never wanted just that. Rather, it is about sex with Tom; since the wilderness trip, Jean believed that for Tom it is, or could be, the same. Another thought falls through him: Have Hugo and Tom been camping? Has Tom zipped their sleeping bags together? Has Hugo counted Tom's freckles and after, did Tom and Hugo swim naked in the sea?

And Jean remembers with a sudden clarity that makes him dizzy why he smashed all the glass in the house when he was eight.

Earlier that day, Jean's father had appeared at his school. Rosa had yet to collect Jean and, besides him, only two other children were left: Arthur, a new boy in the year below, and Libby, who was always left behind. Jean was waiting in the playground alone when he looked up and saw his father there, impossibly tall and impossibly blond, blocking out the sun.

Before then, Jean had only met his father the one time, when he came to visit them at home. It was his blondness that fascinated

Jean, who was aware, even at that age, that his light hair and blue eyes set him apart from Rosa. Her dark looks and foreign accent meant that mothers often confused her for his nanny. Rosa was proud of the way Jean looked. She told him he was lucky. He would grow up to be English and normal. That was the word she used. *Normal.* Except, of course, the opposite was—is—true. Meeting his father, someone who looked so much like him, was more than a relief. That was why Jean could not stop staring, why he reached out to touch his father. His father had brushed Jean off, asking if the boy was a bit funny in the head. Jean was too hurt to respond, and when his father left, he knew he had failed.

It was a shock, then, to see his father at the school gates a few months later. Once again, Jean was struck by the image of him. What if he disappointed him again? But then his father opened his arms and smiled, smiled at Jean.

Jean walked toward him, swelling pride mingling with excitement as his father beckoned. He was scared of his father, but he was also happy. And in his happiness, he was distracted. Which was why he did not notice Arthur, the boy in the year below with the same blond hair and blue eyes, running toward his father, until Arthur was in his father's arms.

Being with Tom and Hugo now, Jean has the same sense of disorientation as he did then, watching his father pick up another little boy from school. Tom and Hugo have forgotten him and are talking about the best way to get the money to the girl, if there's a doctor who will perform the abortion. Hugo says something and Tom laughs, clapping him on the back, and Jean is reminded of the way his father swung Arthur in his arms. It was this, the sight of his father picking up another little boy from school that bubbled up in Jean later, after Rosa had collected him, after he had eaten his snack and drunk his juice, and led him to break one thing after the other, all the glass in the house.

This time, when Tom holds Jean back, Jean strains against him. Tom slaps Jean, telling him to pull his shit together. He presses his arm against Jean's throat and backs him into the sofa.

And did Tom curl his body round Hugo's like a comma, did Hugo lace his fingers between Tom's? Somewhere in the building a pipe shudders to life. Cook will be getting up, so will the first boys going to the farm. The sun streams into the room, lighting them up. Far away there are footsteps, and Hugo is saying something, or is he shouting, or is that the birds outside, the water in the pipes, the hiss of the pan, the squeal of the pigs, all melding together before sliding away, as Jean hears nothing, sees nothing, but what will soon be Tom's face, the pale skin turned a mess of red and brown, crushed petals, rotten twigs, coral in a rockpool.

After Jean hits Tom, once, twice, several things happen: David enters the room and grapples Jean. Tom, the blood running thickly down his face, goes for Jean but is held back by Hugo. Then Hugo is pushed away by David, and now they stand, the three of them, panting in different corners of the room, David in the middle, flapping his arms like a hen. He seems unsure whether to restrain Jean or to help Tom. But the fight has left Jean, just as, when he was eight, the anger spooled out of him. He feels heavy, weighed down by the knowledge that for Tom, for his father, he was not and never will be the real thing. He will only ever be practice.

What the hell is going on here? David says. Well?

There are few things worse than being a faggot, but a snitch is one of them. Jean has never been good at explaining himself. When he was eight, Rosa did not ask and he did not tell her that he had seen his father, knowing it would hurt her. He so successfully buried the knowledge that he forgot about it for years. In the same way, he knows that if he tells David what is going on, he will hurt Tom. Sexual relations between students are strictly forbidden and he knows how important exams are to Tom. Tom spits blood on the carpet. Jean doesn't know how to lie. He never has. Best to stay silent then. To take the heat for the fight. He braces himself for the lecture.

But David straightens, and his voice is strained with a new tension when he says: What's this?

There on the table, the open cough drops tin: the brown baggy, the white square.

Whose tin is this?

Jean looks at Tom, Tom at Jean. Jean can see, now, the hate. He is not sure if it is because he hit Tom or because Tom never cared about him in the first place or because Jean has put Tom in this impossible position. A flicker of doubt flares in him, like when a log from a fire that has long gone out catches the wind, and he wonders if he got it wrong. Was Tom really trying to help him? He remembers again the way Tom cleaned up the glass. The way, not so long ago, Tom kissed him. But this extinguishes as quickly as it rises.

Whose tin is this?

David waits for an answer. Jean knows what Tom will say before he says it. Tom looks at the spots of red that decorate his feet.

Jean's.

Later, on that final night in the wilderness when their bodies were stiff with cold and their throats hoarse from talking, Jean and Tom had walked along the beach, arms wrapped around each other. Jean stopped, crouching by the surf to look at the skeleton of a gull. The bones were bleached white and smoothed by the sun and linked together perfectly, as if the animal had remained untouched. As if nothing and no one had walked this stretch of beach before. It was beautiful, like a necklace, but when Jean picked it up, the skeleton disintegrated, becoming nothing more than a collection of bones.

XII

JEAN TRIES TO COUNT THE COWS AS THEY ZOOM PAST. THEIR mottled brown bodies, their wide pink noses, the morning early but bright around them. As the train speeds through the land, their patches whorl together, like a brush cutting through wet paint. It is a beautiful day, just after seven: the sky is a stretch of blue, the sun a piece of sherbet. Right now, the other boys will be waking up. Jean wonders what will be for breakfast, and then he remembers it is Friday, the best day of the week, when Cook stops experimenting and makes what she knows: sausages, bacon, beans, eggs, mushrooms buttery with garlic, grilled tomatoes, black pudding, golden hash browns. Fried slice, so crispy you could throw it like a Frisbee, the grease sliding down your hands. The boys will wake to the smells of this, the meaty scents wafting through the rooms. Still groggy, they will lurch out of bed, feet shrinking from cold tiles. A splash of water;

some might brush their teeth, most won't bother, pulling on the clothes they've been wearing all week, shorts and sweat-stained T-shirts, hair matted, and along the corridors, the old carpets soft under their feet, the paintings of dukes or earls or whoever used to own Compton Manor looming down at them, the lattice windows creating a pattern of light through which the boys stream, more awake, some pushing and shoving, some racing, toward the main hall. Now the train passes a lake, a wide expanse at the edge of woods. Soon, once breakfast is finished, the boys will clatter through the main hall, out the front door, across the gravel drive, and down one of the two split stone staircases, like a ribbon divided, onto the first of the grass parterres. Will any of them stop there to admire the Diver who rises backward out of the small decorative pond, or will they, most likely, stream past, unseeing because the statue is always there and will continue to be? Down the first parterre and the second, the sculpted green that reminds Jean of a cake, and into the field, their yelps louder, the older ones walking, lighting up the first (or second, or third) fag of the day, the food settled in their stomachs, the nicotine hitting the back of their brains and making their bodies light and sensitive so that when they reach the boating pond, when they strip off, the morning breeze pimpling their flesh, and when they dive into the water, the sting and the cold come as a shock, and they emerge breathless and grinning.

That is how the morning will pass for those boys, Jean thinks, cramped on his train seat. He still has not washed or slept, his mouth is a furball and his eyes like beads on a string. This is how the morning will pass for those boys, and they will not consider it unusual, because it is how the morning will pass for them every day, until one day it does not.

Tom's face looms out of the landscape. Jean balls his fists into his eyes, but this simply makes the image clearer.

Now the fields rise and dip; neat squares cut out and patchworked together. Here the land is not so green, more yellow. In other fields the hay is tall and ready to be cut. Strange to think that Jean walked through land just like this on his way to see Tom. The fields change around him, turning into small, squat gardens, the bland backs of terraced houses revealed like soiled girdles, and there is a road, and a large placard for Piccadilly King Size. And it occurs to Jean that Rosa made a similar journey when she was his age, catching first a train from Berlin to the Hook of Holland, then a boat to Southampton, then another train to London, nothing but her suitcase with her. When she got to England did she, too, stare down at the rows of dirty, terraced houses and pale advertisements and feel as disappointed then as Jean does now? Did she dread it as much. He wonders what David has told her, and quite how angry she will be. He presses his forehead against the glass, his breath steams the outside world into blankness.

When Jean arrives home, Rosa is in the kitchen, something classical blasting out of the radio. The kitchen is on the lower ground floor and stretches along the length of the house: at one end, the velvet sofa, the shelves of books, the high window onto the street through which only pedestrians' feet are visible and the edge of the rhododendron bush, its blooms now a brown mush on the ground; next to the sofa, the record player, the television set, a retro thing from the sixties, the armchair, its springs long gone, its pale linen covering worn and soft. At the other end, the round dining table, above it, the small clay angel that hangs from the conservatory roof on a ribbon, the door to the garden through which Jean can see daisies, dahlias, roses, and, at the far end, the rowan tree. And in the middle, Rosa, bending by the oven, a rich sweetness filling the room.

She is wearing the kimono she has had since forever. The pale blue fabric has faded almost to white and the pattern—two figures standing on a bridge over a pool of water, pink blossom hanging from its arch—is barely distinguishable. As a child, Jean traced the curve of the bridge across her hip, pressing the two rounds of the figures' faces with the pads of his fingers. It was a game he enjoyed, so did Rosa, who would lie there calmly reading him a story. It comes back to him now, and he is caught off guard by the tenderness of it.

Rosa is smaller than he remembers, thinner too. As she bends by the oven, he can see the ridges of her spine. It seems ridiculous that this frail, old woman (Rosa, in her fifties, is the same age as some of the other boys' grandmothers) should loom so large in his mind. When she turns and sees him, her mouth puckering to an *O*, her hand pressing against the kitchen counter to hold her up, he suspects she is going to drop the tray—and he almost rushes forward to help her, scared she will hurt herself. Her surprise is as evident as his own: clearly, she was not expecting him. But she regains her balance, propping herself on the counter, and he pours himself a glass of water, leaning against the sink, feeling the cool water slide down his gullet. They stand like that, at other ends of the room, Jean with his water, Rosa with her cakes, observing each other.

Her hair has grown long; this new hairstyle in line with the times (she has also cut a fringe), rather than making her seem more stylish, has the adverse effect. Her greys are more pronounced and beyond the snap of her collarbone the locks thin to wispy strands. How much time has passed since he last saw her? Two months, three, more? She has only loosely tied the kimono and underneath Jean can see the thin fabric of her cotton nightgown. It is one of those old numbers, bought from a *brocante* in France: the torn, embroidered neckline scoops low on her front, and the hem cuts off somewhere high on her legs. She is barefoot.

A few quick movements with her eyes and she takes him in. He imagines what she sees—unwashed hair, deeply tanned skin, faded, dirty jeans, leather jacket, boots. Jean, fully clothed as he is, feels like he has disturbed her in some deeply private ritual. Rosa puts the tray down to retie the kimono, tugging the cord tight around her midriff and closing the gaps at neck and thigh. He waits for her to make some comment: about his appearance, about his arrival, but instead she turns down the radio and the sudden change in volume makes Jean's stomach lurch. The whole room seems to be holding its breath. As Rosa deftly pops out the cakes onto a wire rack, she says:

I didn't hear you come in.

Her voice is light, conversational, as if she genuinely is surprised. Jean drinks another glass of water; the second is not as delicious as the first and there is a lump in his throat that makes it hard to swallow. This is not what he expected. When he was last home at Easter, he went to a party, and it was early morning by the time he got home. He was careful to be as quiet as possible, entering by the lower ground level door (the same through which he came today) that opens straight into the kitchen, rather than by the main door of the upper ground level, where Rosa's studio is. He was standing by the sink, as he is now, downing a few glasses of water, as he has just done, when the plate whizzed by his ear.

Jean isn't sure if she meant to miss or if Rosa just has a bad throw; certainly, he had to duck for the second one. She was in her winter robe then, which is made of wool, and gave Jean the impression of a freshly shorn sheep, her bare feet stepping confidently across the room despite the shards of porcelain. She used one hand to hold the stack of plates, the other to fling them from an ever-decreasing distance. He managed, on her fourth attempt, to grab her wrists, the remaining plates falling with a clatter to the floor. Rosa rested her trembling head against his chest.

It is a shock, then, to find her baking, his favourite confectionary no less—to be confronted with this mild, restrained version of his mother. To remember a softness about her; as a little boy, stretched across her midriff, the kimono soft beneath his cheek, the peace of her voice. Jean is wary, choosing not to reply—it wasn't a question anyway—but instead saying, That smells good.

They're not as crisp as usual, Rosa squishes a sponge between her fingers before dropping it again. Fuck.

Rosa half smiles at him, a kind of grimace, bringing him into the complicity of her mistake. A smile that says, Classic impatient me, burning myself. Jean blinks back. There is a small part of him that continues to hope—hope that David has not yet called her, that she does not yet know, but also that things could be different, better. It is this part of him that half smiles back, self-consciously commiserating with her.

They never, Rosa says briskly, turning back to the cakes, slight colour in her cheeks, Turn out the same.

She seems equally self-conscious, equally cautious. This fortifies Jean and makes him bold enough to say,

They look great.

To which Rosa gives a small shrug, a show of modesty that tells him she is pleased and tells him he has more time. Jean will need to invent something, eventually, once Rosa asks him why he is home. He will tell her he is back for the weekend to study, then figure out his next moves. But right now, as he watches Rosa pick up a cake, sniff it, turn her mouth down in a show of appreciation, why Jean is back does not seem pressing. What is pressing is his need to sleep, eat—those cakes do smell good—wash. His body, which has been tense since the early hours, relaxes.

I hope they crisp as they cool, Rosa says.

And Jean, in his relief, almost shouts with enthusiasm, I'm sure they will.

He misjudges: the volume and pitch of his voice make Rosa flinch. Her mouth hardens, her shoulders tense, and she turns away from him. The nausea that has bubbled low in his belly since this morning rises again. The pain in his neck returns. His upper back feels like someone has secured a clamp to it and is twisting tighter. Are Rosa's hands shaking? It occurs to Jean that it is strange to find Rosa here, in the kitchen, on a Friday morning, waiting for him. As if reading his mind she says:

I don't teach on Fridays. But when I go in on Monday, I can ask about a job.

With this, she turns to the oven, and the relief Jean felt spirals out of him. As Rosa produces another tray of madeleines, she tells him there is a janitor position available. Jean pinches the inside of his arm to calm himself down. Rosa pops the second batch of madeleines onto the tray, which is overcrowded, and pulls out another tray, this time with financiers.

It is not ideal, she says, she was hoping for a technician job, but what with the recession it's as good a start as any. After the financiers come puff pastries, their tops cracked and molten with sugar. If Jean works at the school for a year, then he will be eligible for employee benefits. It is hot, despite the open garden doors. And it is clear, as Rosa reaches deep into the oven and whips out, with a flourish, an apricot frangipane tart, as she tells him about the pension and the free night classes, the heat and the sweetness increasing with her volume and pitch, and as she bangs the oven door shut with her heel, that Rosa knows.

Of course she knows. It is already ten in the morning, hours since Jean sat in David's office, blinking past the headmaster's bald head at the lattice windows to the blue outside. David himself was puce and sweat ran in rivulets down his cheeks. He couldn't sit down but instead paced, one hand behind his back, the other making flourishes for emphasis. He warned Jean, he warned him. Another episode and Jean would be out. David stamped his foot, and his whole demeanour was so much like that of an angry headmaster in a sketch (Groucho Marx waddled into Jean's mind) that Jean found it hard to take him seriously. The reality was serious though. What was happening around and to Jean was seriously happening. And this episode wasn't like the others, was it? Jean may have hit Tom, but it wasn't the violent outburst for which Jean was kicked out—although it certainly contributed. Rather, it was the cough drops tin.

Indeed, Rosa continues, smoothing the front of her kimono, picking a stray hair from her mouth and speaking in a low, quick voice, if Jean does the night classes, he can develop his sculpture and eventually go to art school. She takes a tea towel and twists it into a taut rope, the muscles in her forearms straining with the effort. The music has stopped, and the presenter is saying something, his low, sonorous voice mixing with the insistent drone of building works outside and making it hard for Jean to concentrate. Underneath the sweet is a dank smell that turns Jean's stomach. Is Rosa steaming an entire salmon? There are herbs on the counter, chopped and fragrant, and in a bowl, what looks like hollandaise. Most art schools don't even require exams, Rosa says, opening the fish kettle and releasing a pungent cloud into the already sweltering room. It doesn't matter that Jean is seventeen without a single qualification or any consistent schooling.

Jean knew the rules about drugs, David said, thrusting the tin under Jean's nose, even though Jean already knew what sat there. The neat brown packet next to the bright white baggy. There was a desperation in the headmaster's voice, as if he wanted Jean to refute the evidence. At that point Jean could have—he could have said the drugs weren't his, that Charles gave them to Hugo who gave them to Tom who gave them to him. Which was partly true. But Charles wasn't there anymore; why would David believe Jean over Hugo? And of course, there was Theo—Jean recalled, as he sat staring at the stains between the headmaster's teeth, the first time he met Theo, offering him a joint, the way the other boy had stiffened and refused. The grass, at least, was Jean's.

Now Rosa stirs the herbs into the hollandaise, now spears a potato bubbling away on the stove, now turns a bowl onto the wooden countertop and begins kneading frantically. Music on the radio again, but this time something frenetic and bopping, Duke Ellington, maybe, which adds a manic layer to the scene in the kitchen. He imagines Rosa a few hours ago, the sunlight leaking around the blinds, her hair a mess, the dialling tone bleating from the phone still in her hand. Knowing she wouldn't sleep, she headed straight for the kitchen—or did she try to paint first?—reaching for the eggs and cracking them into a bowl. Her need to do something pathological, she wouldn't stop cooking until the kitchen was full.

If he does want to get an O-level or two, she says now, there is a college nearby where he can sit them. But that will cost.

Jean should be grateful that Rosa is not shouting or throwing things, that she is offering him a solution. Because Rosa is, he knows, just trying to help. But rather than assuage him, her manic cooking and her torrent of speech—she is saying now that she'd like to redo her studio, and there are a few bits around the house that need work, and she'd pay him, he'd like that wouldn't he, her voice rapping in time with the wild beat of the music—make him feel as if the walls are closing in steadily around him.

Framed prints, illustrations from Rosa's first big children's book for which she used Jean as a model, cover the kitchen. Through the open doors, at the back of the garden the rowan tree stands, its blooms long gone and replaced with drooping, oval leaves. From where Jean is, he can see little clusters of unripe berries. It is in the garden where he has always been happiest. When he was younger there was a sandpit, and he could spend hours making his own worlds. Or he would stomp around the flower beds, pressing firm bulbs into the giving ground. Using his own miniature can, the split sprinkle of water moistening the bright flowers and bending leaves below.

Now Jean remembers how bored he was standing on the lawn while Rosa sketched him. She wouldn't let him tend to the flowers or play in the sandpit; if he moved at all, she got annoyed. He has always hated the illustrations on the walls, embarrassed by the images of himself that adorn the house. But as he looks at them now, each image reflecting and distorting the sunny garden opposite, they seem to represent something more menacing than childhood humiliation. Jean has the sense that he is, and always has been, trapped. And as Rosa continues to talk, over and through him, as if he is not there, as if he has no thoughts or plans of his own, he has the sense that this is exactly what she wants. But why does he not say anything?

Just like when he sat in the headmaster's office, he was silent. He could have tried to argue with David. Jean might have thrown Hugo, Theo, Charles under the bus, had Tom not told David the tin was Jean's.

Jean tries to pinpoint the exact moment he lost Tom. Was it when he hit Tom, square in the mouth, or was it before that? Was it when Jean asked him to come with him to China, or when he pretended to eat hemlock, or before that, when he let Tom fuck him, or even before that, before he knew of Tom's existence, when Jean was crouched in the pig pen, cleaning out the shit. Tom was already lost to Jean because Jean was always going to fuck it up.

It was this certainty, the certainty that Tom had not just betrayed Jean, but that Jean deserved it, that kept him quiet in the headmaster's office. And it is this same knowledge—the knowledge that there is something wrong with him—that keeps Jean silent now, so that when Rosa delineates all the things she'd like done in the house, saying that really, his coming home is a good thing, how helpful Jean can be, he does not resist. Rather, he feels the inevitability of having his life sketched out by Rosa.

Although everything in his body screams no, he feels himself accepting it. It is fitting, somehow, this punishment. Jean tried to strike out and look where it got him, right back here, with nothing more than a broken heart. Rosa seems to sense Jean's acquiescence because she stops talking and gives him that same flat grimace, as if to say, What else is there?

From the radio comes the muffled sound of applause, the commentator says something and into the space the first bars of a new song trickle. Softly at first, the initial chords distorted by static, then, when the voice starts, stronger, echoing through the room. It takes Jean a second to recognise what the song is and who is singing it. Micky's voice, throaty and light, the spare accompaniment of his piano, moves about the kitchen, filling it like a ghost. As if Jean didn't feel bad enough already, here it is, "Boy in Space," his song, their song. Micky sings about two inseparable friends roaming the streets, their love for each other warming them against the winter frost, cooling them in the summer heat. Jean's already low mood sinks further as he is reminded of Micky who, like Tom, is another person Jean pushed away.

But then Rosa gives a little gasp and tells Jean in a rush that Michael left a few weeks ago. And wouldn't it be a good idea if, in the interim between applying for the janitor position at the school—no wait, wait, perhaps *instead* of applying for the janitor position, he should start his own business? She is sure that the new neighbours, a lovely older couple with no children, will want some work done on the house.

Especially to that god-awful hellhole, Rosa laughs, and Jean is reminded of the aubergine living room, the red hallway, the chrome kitchen. Back down on the tiger rug, staring at the dark ceiling above him, while Micky, playing his piano, sang about boys who turn trash into treasure.

Just as Micky does now, his voice gaining in pitch and volume, the small radio blasting into the room. He describes the two boys climbing over mounds of rubble, their hands grubby, their hearts listless. The boys find an old metal drum and drag it into the garden, along with other foraged items. They are covered in dirt, they have nothing else to play with, but the thing they make is spectacular.

Now Rosa is listing everything *she* would get redone in Micky's house, starting with repainting the hallway. Still, she does not consciously seem to notice the song.

Jean stares at her, waiting for her to clock it. A little disbelieving that she can talk about Micky, about his home, when she knows—surely, she must know—what Micky, what that house, means to Jean. And now Micky describes two tin lids, bent into wings; and now an empty bucket of paint for a helmet and Jean is reminded, lurchingly, of being a child and telling Micky about the things he found in the bombed-out toy factory behind the house. And now Rosa is saying she would burn the furniture. And Jean wonders: Does she *not* know?

The song shifts gear, changing from major to minor, as Micky sings about the night that descends. One boy is asleep in a warm bed, having been fed and safely tucked in, while the other lies awake, hungry and alone. His mother has not come home, and he is too embarrassed to tell his friend. Instead, he creeps out into the inky blackness and climbs into the spaceship they created, warmed by the happy memories of earlier that day.

Something shifts in Jean too. When he was younger, he used

to find these lyrics comforting: to him, the spaceship was Micky's home, he the little boy safely in it. And when the starlight fell from the sky, it was Micky, offering Jean refuge. But now the words take on new meaning.

And the art! Rosa is saying. Don't even get me started on the art.

And in the song: a star falls, touching the tin roof, setting it ablaze.

Now the boy is alone in his spaceship, the starlight casting him first in brilliance, then in shadow, as he hurtles through the sky. And now Micky is washing Jean's hair in the wide, marble tub. Each time the soap suds sting Jean's eyes, Micky wipes them away. And now Jean is on his back in the dirt, Tom red-faced and pounding above. Jean is on his knees in a dirty bathroom stall in France. And the boy looks into the starlight, his face lit up. He is afraid, but he is also powerless to stop what happens next; he is sucked into the dark like an ant from a hole.

Last August, the last time they saw each other, Micky told Jean he missed him. Jean understands why, now, instead of making him glow, it snapped something inside. Although he didn't make the connection at the time, Jean's episode with the Italian man changed everything. What had once seemed full of magical potential became sad and, truthfully, disgusting. The maroon silk sheets, the rooms painted aubergine, orange, and yellow, the record player, the talk about love and peace and children. This song. Jean was angry at Micky, angry for making him feel special, for making him want—what? And he was angry at himself. Angry that he had fallen for it, yes, but also that he now saw through it. That is why he hit Micky last August. That is why now, as the song dips and the spaceship rattles, Jean has the sensation of being turned inside out, used in a way he cannot name, and he hates Micky all over again.

Rosa claps her hands enthusiastically. Jean's Jobs! That could be the name of his business. He could go from door to door, certainly the street has changed, plenty of people with money these days. Just think, she says, They'd both be painters!

Then a new thought: Maybe she was never oblivious. Maybe she knew what was going on—what is going on right now—but doesn't care. In Rosa's enthusiasm she hits the edge of the cooling tray and knocks one of the cakes to the floor, and Jean's anger at Micky, his disgust at himself, now turn toward her. No wonder Jean is so fucked up.

He wants to hurt her, to punish her and by doing so rid himself of the tarnish he feels covered in. To remove the bad part. There is a knife on the draining board. Small, meant for cutting apples, but sharp. He imagines picking it up.

But then Rosa stands, holding the retrieved cake in her hand with a triumphant, Got it! The song dips, reverting to the chorus. The two boys together, triumphant on a mound of concrete. The one boy looking down from space, calling to his friend.

Jean is disoriented just as, when standing on the tube platform, the sensation to jump overwhelms him and then passes, and he is faced with the possibility of his near miss. Rosa makes a movement forward, then holds herself back, unsure. She wants to come to him, Jean realises, but she is afraid. Something of Jean's feeling must be written on his face because Rosa says:

Darling, oh darling.

Jean is afraid too. Rosa loves him. She is trying to help but she cannot. She never could, and she will never be able to.

The boys will have finished their swim by now. The younger ones will be lying in the fields, the sun carving an arc across the sky, the older boys will have returned to the billiard room. There will be fish and chips for lunch, the fish brought fresh from the coast that morning, the chips hand cut. And will they, as they sit around the table, be discussing not Charles's disappearance, but Jean's? Will Hugo tell them that the retard, the Yid, the faggot had a full-on breakdown? And will Tom agree, and will Tom laugh? Or will Tom, as he has done before, tell Hugo to be quiet? Other things: the way Tom gripped Jean's hip bone, the way he nuzzled close to him in his sleep, the way he smiled, openly, at Jean's jokes.

Outside it is hot and still. It seems to Jean that his song is playing from every window in the street. Jean stands at the base of the stone steps, slanted and green from use and age. How many times has he stood here like this, waiting to emerge into the world above? He likes this entrance because it is on the lower ground floor, because he must climb into the world, as if emerging from hell. He will miss that, if nothing else. Above him the pavement appears like a ridge on a cliff, and as Jean ascends the steps, he feels like he is climbing a mountain. He knows he will not come home again. When he walks away, he will leave everything behind.

He will not come back to the house: the bay window upstairs, the barred window below. The rows of bookshelves in the living room, the lamp, the floorboards, the notches on the wall from where he has grown, the corner cupboard with the good china, the back cupboard with the enamel, the heavy-bottomed pans, the Dutch oven, the main oven, the grill, the one hundred egg cups, the paintbrushes, the images of himself, the drawers of ticket stubs, the bathroom and its hessian carpet. His room. The boxing bag, the Bruce Lee poster, the Cézanne postcard, the mattress on the floor.

Other things he will not see again: the art room, with its stained glass windows, the light falling across the floorboards in yellow, red, purple, blue. The billiard room, with the threadbare rug, the cases of books. The dormitories, beds stacked at awkward angles to fit the odd-shaped rooms. The corridors, late in the afternoon, sunlight illuminating the dust particles. The bathroom with its yellow tiles. The showers; the kitchen; the gardens; the staircases, their uneven stairs; the garage; the Tuscan arches; the jasmine; the ornamental garden; the ratty sofa, threadbare, stuffing coming out; the collection of marble eggs; the suit of armour; the rabbit hutches; the chicken coop; the pigs; the barn; the hay; the fence; the gravel drive; even the empty swimming pool; the fire pit; the back field; the lower field; the woods; the lake; the clearing.

As he crosses the threshold, it will be as if these things cease to exist; or rather, belong to someone else. Maybe the boys will not be discussing him at all, having already forgotten he was there. Maybe Tom is thinking about him right now. Maybe Tom loved him.

Micky's final notes are born on a light breeze. The triumphant rise and the sudden, swift dip into a different key, the petering out and the gentle, soft notes that signal the end. It is beautiful; it always has been. He is thirteen again, hearing the song for the first time, and a sudden spark of joy lights in him. Perhaps there is another, third meaning to the song. One that has nothing to do with Micky.

There are so many places he can go: houses that lie empty just around the corner, parties that extend through the week, and other places, too, that have nothing to do with people. Bruce Lee would say that this life is the material that holds us back; it is the next that counts.

The song, really, speaks of unending promises. Visions of Jean's potential futures come to him. He is a monk, flying through the air; he is a meditation master, still as a reed; he is a fisherman; a nomad, moving through the land he knows by touch. He is a taxi driver, the knowledge of London's streets embedded in his body like veins. He is a boxer. He is a poet. He is moving through houses with empty rooms; he is living in a tent; he is somewhere on the other side of the world speaking a foreign language.

The boys will be leaving the classroom now, stretching their legs as they walk along the field, the sun heating their foreheads. The sun is bright and hot on Jean's forehead, and he feels giddy as he mounts the final step and looks down the street. He is not standing on Clemens Gardens, Holland Park, but rather, on the peak of a Tian Shan mountain in China. Rosa says something, somewhere far behind him—is it a question, is it a demand?—but he is no longer listening.

He steps out, walking in time with the music. Around him the light falls through the plane trees, dappling his face and boots, so he feels like he is moving through something more substantial than air. The point is it is still summer and will continue to be for some time.

ACKNOWLEDGMENTS

This novel has taken years to write and gone through many iterations. Thank you, Emma, Jay, and Mark for your generosity and time when I was learning to write. Mary and Carolyn, thank you for your compassion, humour, and art, and for your sustaining friendship. Thank you especially to my mother, who has been unfaltering in her support, sharing her wisdom. I am in awe of your strength and your ability to find joy in moments of pain. This is also something that comes from my grandmother, whom I miss every day. Fiercely committed to the people she loved and the idea of a fairer world, she taught me to balance wit with warmth, and to take the work, not oneself, seriously.

Thank you to my US editor, Jill Bialosky, for plucking what became this novel from something more unwieldy. Working with you made a daunting task exciting and guided me when I was otherwise lost. Thank you to my UK editor, Marigold

Atkey, for your infectious enthusiasm, eagle-eyed observations and dedication. I am grateful to everyone at Norton and Daunt: to Laura Mucha for steering me through the publishing process; to my copyeditor, Jodi Hughes, and my proofreader, Lynne Cannon Menges, for seeing what I was otherwise blind to; to my publicity and marketing teams, Gabby Nugent, Meredith McGinnis, and Jimena Gorráez, for shepherding this book, and myself, into the world; and to my designers, Jason Heuer and Kishan Rajani, for the most beautiful covers. Thank you to Yann Faucher, Charles Odell, and Millenium Images for the stunning photographs. Thank you to my wonderful production team: Rebecca Munro, Ramona Wilkes, Chris Welch, Becca Calf, and Marsha Swan. Thank you to all the booksellers who have sold a copy of this book; and anyone who has bought one.

Thank you to my agent, Emma Paterson, for bearing with me and in whose company I came of age, as a writer and a person. Thank you to Lisa Baker, Anna Hall, the foreign rights and accounts teams, and everyone at Aitken Alexander for your hard work.

Without my teachers, this novel would not exist. Thank you to Brandon Taylor for teaching me the importance of boredom, manners, and a long chapter; thank you to Garth Greenwell for the transcendent sentences and the sex writing, and for your compassion; thank you to Jeffrey Eugenides for the expansive conversations and literary grounding. Thank you to Katie Kitamura for your care and crucial insight. Thank you to Jonathan Safran Foer for going above and beyond: not only for the generous edits and continued support but, also, for the wonderful piñata. Thank you to Diana Evans, Tom Lee, Rachel Seiffert, and Ben Markovits for helping me find a way in. To my other teachers—Ross Raisin, Francis Spufford, Hari Kunzru, Raven Leilani, Darin Strauss, Sally Wen Mao—I have taken something from each of your classes. Thank you, Jackie Tasioulas, Fred Parker, Anne Stillman, Deborah Bowman, and, especially, Tamara Follini, for your commitment and for instilling in me the joy of books. Thank you to Peter Straus, Georgia Garrett, and everyone at RCW for teaching me the drafting needed to write one. Thank you to Deborah Landau, Zachary Sussman, Sebastian Doherty, and the whole team with the NYU Creative Writing Program for crafting a generative and nourishing environment. To all the writers and artists, living and dead, on whose work I have feasted, and of which there are too many to name, thank you.

To my peers, thank you for reading generously and plentifully. Natalie and Susannah, thank you for feeding my heart, mind, and, often, my belly. Thank you, Mimi, for your wicked intelligence and pure grace. Thank you, August, your solidarity kept me going. And thank you, Esme, for being my biggest cheerleader. Thank you, Euan, for describing formative encounters; and thank you, Fergus, for checking to make sure my scenes made sense. Thank you all for being my family while I lived alone in another country—and to Sam, Eli, Frankie, Josh, Ali, and the extended Birnbaum family—and remaining so, now that I am gone. Thank you to Katy and to all my early readers, of this work and of others. Thank you, Rosie, for letting me follow in your footsteps; Julia for reading the first, messiest draft; and Rowan for reading a later, still messy, draft, and who has always been there. Thank you, Tyro, for your beautiful eye and Lettice for your wise counsel. Daisy and Pandora, thank you for your unwavering camaraderie. Thank you, Dylan, for your blood-thirsty bunnies. To all my friends, thank you for picking up the phone; you are each a lifeline in this stormy living. Thank you to everyone who has listened to me and spoken with me, encouraged, advised and helped me.

Thank you to my sister, my first love and inspiration, who made writing feel possible. Thank you for holding me high, even if you felt low, and for being the other half of my brain. Thank you to my father, my first teacher and ongoing guide. Thank you for reading everything and for keeping me sharp. Thank you to my brother for heartening my soul. Thank you, Auntie Annie, for the courage and the cold-water swims. Thank you, Nana, for your spirit. Thank you, Jenni, for the love. Thank you to Bríd and John for your kindness and your dinner table. Thank you to my whole family for supporting me always.

Thank you to Sophie Crawford for running Patterned Ground where I read an embryonic sample of this novel; and to all the spaces that let you try and fail. Thank you to Goldsmiths for letting me experiment and thank you to the institutions and organisations whose crucial support made this book possible: Isaac Arthur Green Fellowship, Goethe Institut, Genesis Emerging Writers' Programme, Jill Davis Fellowship, Global Research Initiative (GRI) NYU Research Fellowship.

Thank you to the breast cancer teams at Homerton and St. Bart's.

Oisín, thank you for everything.